Picture Perfect Bride

Picture Perfect Bride

A Cupid's Corner Romance

Laurie LeClair

TULE
PUBLISHING

Dedication

To my sweet husband, Jim LeClair. Thank you for this wonderful journey of love and laughter and unshakable belief in us. You and me, babe. Always.

Prologue

ADAM LARSON TOSSED down his pencil. It hit the pad he'd scribbled figures on with a dull thud. Leaning back, his chair squeaked. *Need to fix that.* The noise echoed in the quiet, efficient construction trailer brightened by the overhead fluorescent lighting.

He rubbed his hand over his face and then gazed around at the three other desks—their occupants sane enough to leave for the weekend already. Unrolled blueprints covered the main table. A row of corkboards with haphazard papers and safety rules pinned on them and write on wipe off boards filled with diagrams and notes of present and future jobs hung on nearly every inch of the walls.

The sudden ring of his desk phone jolted him.

He snatched it up. "Larson here."

"I knew you'd be there."

He grinned at his executive assistant's exasperated tone. "Mrs. Sanderson, that's funny, because I knew you'd be calling."

"So, why are you still there?"

"I had to answer the phone, didn't I?"

She chuckled. "Oh, what am I going to do with you? Look, in roughly ten minutes there will be a knock on the door. Answer it."

"Bossy. What is it? A singing gram?" He was definitely punchy after the long work week. They'd come in before deadline and under budget—two of his favorite things as the owner of the company. He let his staff and crew knock off hours earlier as a small reward. He stayed working on the next project—estimates, materials, and a list of contractors needed.

"Your dinner. Thank me later."

Adam sighed. "A bonus or a vacation?" This woman was a treasure.

"You just gave me both. It was great to visit with your mom and dad again in Florida. My kids and grandkids had lots of fun at the beach…" In the background, excited voices rushed down the line. "Speaking of which, that's them now storming in. Game night."

"Go. I'll be fine."

"That's debatable."

"See you Monday morning." Adam hung up, shaking his head.

Without Mrs. Sanderson, who hired him nearly six years ago for his first real, full-time construction job, taught him the inside out of the business—even after he jumped to another firm for a promotion and better pay—and then agreed to join him when he started his own, he'd never have come so far so fast.

With drive and determination, he'd beaten the odds of a

predetermined outcome for the kid from the wrong side of the tracks.

He'd found his niche in the crowded construction business. He made a very good living out of renovating old, broken down, neglected buildings and houses, pumping new life into them. A fixer, as Mrs. Sanderson dubbed him.

When he heard the low hum of the engine and the tires crunching on the gravel stones drawing near, he shoved back from his chair. He got to the door at the same time the rapid knock sounded.

Adam opened it to find the delivery driver holding the large paper sack with the high-end, award-winning restaurant logo stamped on the side. "Afternoon."

"Closer to evening." The older guy nodded to the sun low in the sky.

The warm orange ball shimmered in the distance. It reminded Adam how much time he'd lost today. Again.

"What do I owe you?" He grabbed for his wallet out of the back pocket of his jeans.

"It's paid for."

"Tip?" He pulled out some bills.

"Taken care of already." The middle-aged man grinned as he handed over the bagged meal. "Over thirty percent. The best kind."

Mrs. Sanderson thought of everything. "Thanks. Have a good one."

Adam waited there on the small landing, as the guy backed out in his blue compact car, and watched the glowing sun.

It tumbled Adam back in time when he was a teenager. He stood transfixed at the reminder of how happy and satisfied he'd been after finishing up work on Pickens farm, sitting in the open door of the hay loft to stare at the gorgeous sunsets—precious moments in his hometown of Cupid's Corner, a place he'd turned his back on over six years ago.

He'd hurt so many people, especially...

"Molly." His heart squeezed in his chest.

He drew in a deep breath, still aching.

Pulling himself away from the view and from his guilt, he returned to his desk with the slam of the door still rattling on its hinges.

His mind drifted as he ate the delicious steak dinner. The tug of his computer was too much to deny. He powered it up, went online, and then debated on his next move.

Adam went there. He clicked on the saved link for *Cupid's Corner Gazette*, swallowing hard as the memories of simpler, sweeter times hit. A low, dull ache ribboned through him.

You gave it up. Why the pull back?

The familiar red banner and logo for the paper popped up. A tug of pride mixed with a bout of regret for not being a part of it any longer whispered through him. Adam scrolled down and stopped dead in his tracks.

"Pickens's barn!" The two pictures of the recent damage to the building grabbed his attention first. He quickly read the article on the dismal outlook. His heart sank. "Mr. Pickens, no. Don't sell. Not to them for a housing development." Adam had visions of the quaint family farm wiped out down to the dirt.

He'd worked in the business long enough to know these kind of developers destroyed the old and replaced it with brand-spanking-new houses stuffed side by side together. The hill where the farm sat was prime property. There might be a fancy golf course involved to make it even more desirable to lure in big money outsiders.

A sickening sensation dropped in his belly, cold and hard.

Going back to the pictures, his mouth dried. He gulped, but his throat turned to scratchy sandpaper. The byline. "Molly McCleary." His heartbeat hammered. "She never married?"

Staring at her name one letter at a time to imprint it again, Adam allowed the enormity of what he'd done to her seep into all the places he'd set up roadblocks for so long. Because trying to hold it back for years hadn't done a thing for his conscience; it still plagued him, always on the edges of his thoughts—burning and itching to break through.

He'd walked away to give her a chance. Something more. Something better.

Had she even come close to getting it?

She deserved happiness. She deserved to live her dreams—all the ones she longed for and told him about— not have a tiny byline on their small hometown newspaper.

"Did I ruin everything for you?" Adam's voice cracked.

He glanced at her name, the damaged barn photos, and then back again. His mind clicked with thoughts and possibilities, connecting the two broken pieces into one whole.

"Can I really do this?"

I'm a fixer, aren't I?

Adam thrived on repairing and patching things together to make them come alive again. Buildings, yes. Broken dreams? Not so much.

He'd righted most of the wrongs in his life, except one. *Molly.*

"Did you...ever forgive me?" Deep down, he hadn't even forgiven himself, so most likely she hadn't, either. "Can I fix this? Can I make this right for you?"

As he talked out loud in the eerie quiet, a plan began to form to give her back a little bit of what he'd taken away...

Chapter One

*M*Y NAME IS *Molly McCleary and I'm a recovering hopeless romantic.*

"Yep, that's me." Molly raised her professional camera, adjusted the long lens, framed the shot, and then snapped the image. The young, recently engaged couple gazed longingly at each other and held hands on the grass-covered area in front of the calm, soothing lapping water of the pond.

Gorgeous blonde hair streamed down the girl's back. His wavy, slightly darker shade complemented the image. They'd opted for casual, cool. A flirty white dress for her and his white shirt paired with brand-new jeans proved a natural fit in the picturesque setting and suited their personalities. Tall and fit and madly in tune with the slightest gesture or touch, the camera loved them. They could have been models. Of course, they were silly and excited and caught up in their engagement photos.

Lost. Oblivious to even Molly.

"And that's the way it should be." Molly sucked in a tiny, painful breath.

Behind them, the early morning sun skimmed the backdrop of Cupid's Corner Pond, making the water appear a shimmering gold sheen. She waited a beat for the sparkling diamond effect and then snapped a half dozen times.

"Perfect silhouette."

Young love. High school sweetheart love.

That was me once. Until it wasn't.

Her chest squeezed. Molly thrust away the aching sweep of envy.

"All right now." She cleared her throat to choke past the thick lump there. "Just like we talked about. Slowly lean in until that brief kiss as I take another round."

They didn't answer; however, they did follow her instructions. Molly's skin prickled with goosebumps as a sudden breeze brushed her arms, but the chilly early morning April temps did nothing to deter the couple's devotion to the task at hand.

Molly barely touched the shutter release button, taking several shots in rapid succession. "Kyle, shift your left shoulder back just a tad, slow and easy. Opens up the stance. That's it."

The couple took direction well as she gently shifted and repositioned them for the next hour. The lush scent of freshly mowed grass and blooming flowers filled the air, making it heighten Molly's senses even more.

Spring, one of her favorite times of the year, promised hope and renewal, two things she longed for right about now.

Only she didn't stand a chance at much of anything with the approaching wedding season hanging over her head.

My kryptonite.

"All right, Kyra, the last one."

The girl giggled and tugged Kyle's hand as she rushed to the next spot. The obligatory one for their hometown of Cupid's Corner—on the small arched wooden bridge stretching from one edge of the water to the other and designed with iron hearts and topped with wood railings—finished up the sunrise session.

"Maybe I should have rented a boat to stand up in, so I could have gotten them straight on." Molly's doubts snuck up on her, leaving her questioning her abilities. Anything remotely related to that wedding curse that hung over her head instilled hesitancy inside her.

She pressed the bubble of anxiety down deep inside. Taking photographs—first of school kids for the last half a dozen years and then for certain friends and special occasions and mostly of her beloved landscapes and buildings—she'd stockpiled a pretty impressive portfolio.

Few had seen it. Her best friend, Gemma, for one. Molly's older brother, Sean, had championed her and even gave all of her deposit for her photography studio a few months ago.

They believe in me. Why can't I?

"That's a wrap, as they say." Molly waved over the sweet couple before taking down the adjustable tripod and looping the strap for her camera back over her neck. "You're gonna love them."

"Really?" Kyra giggled. "Can we take a peek?"

There was something about the girl's enthusiasm that

reminded Molly of herself nearly six years ago. Another sharp tug ripped through her heart.

"One today. The rest when you come back to my shop in a few days." Looking at the digital images, Molly clicked through until she found a good one. "This might be the image for your save-the-date cards." She turned the camera so they could see the LCD screen.

They both gasped.

"That's awesome!" Kyle hugged Kyra from behind and kissed her on the cheek, imitating the picture of them on the bridge.

She squealed. "Molly, it's so adorable. I can't wait to show my girlfriends." Without warning, Kyra wrapped her arms around Molly and hugged her tight, all the while still laughing in her ear.

Going deaf now. "Ah, you're welcome." Molly held herself stiff and still and imagined the pressure of the camera between them would leave an imprint on her chest for a month or five. *Yep, the headlines would read, she'd died with her beloved camera imbedded in her flesh.* Anyone who knew her wouldn't be at all surprised by that one. "Owie."

Thankfully, Kyra pulled away. "Sorry. I got carried away."

Kyle chuckled. "She gets that way. Anything about the wedding and she gets giggly. Isn't it so cute?"

"Very." Molly hoped it came out sincere, even when she was kicking herself for agreeing to this shoot. *Sugary sweet and bad for me.*

"Of course, the wedding." Kyra nudged her forehead

with the palm of her hand. "You'll do it, right? You're the best in town."

"Ah, I hate to tell you this, but I'm the *only* one in town."

"So you know how special Cupid's Corner is. We're going with a late June wedding."

"Yeah, first graduation, then the wedding, honeymoon, and then we're off to college. Can you believe it?" Kyle smiled even through the slightly dazed look in his brown eyes.

"It's a lot to take in." Molly swallowed hard. *This could have been my life. If only...* She shook her head. "Look, the time. You'll be late for school if I keep you any longer."

They groaned in unison. In a moment, they were at the base of a nearby ten-foot-tall metal lamp with intricate hearts swirling beneath the lantern, gathering their stuffed backpacks.

"Come by Thursday after track practice. I'll have the pictures ready and you can tell me how many copies you want."

"Thanks!" Again they spoke in unison. Hand in hand, they half raced up the hill.

That was when Molly sensed someone off to her left, sitting on the back of the wooden bench. "Hey, Gemma." But her best friend's name stuck in her parched throat. She'd witnessed it. Ugh!

So lost in the angles and lighting—shifting her black shade umbrella around to block a glare—she'd missed the approach of her friend.

Dragging her feet, Molly joined her buddy and hiked

herself up beside her, butt on the back of the bench and her booted feet flat on the seat. She rested the tripod against the side of the seat. She fiddled with her camera, avoiding meeting her friend's sharp-eyed gaze. "You saw that."

"Pretty cute, aren't they?"

"So I've heard." But that wasn't the last of this quivery conversation. Molly scooped up her denim jacket from where it was draped over the arm of the bench and yanked it on. Another layer of protection coming right up.

"You're going through with the wedding phase, aren't you? I mean, your brother and mine, too."

They'd been besties since Molly was five going on six when her family moved to Cupid's Corner. Repeating kindergarten wasn't nearly as bad in a new town. And, on that very first day, Gemma plunked herself down in a seat next to her and made Molly pinkie swear they'd be best friends for life.

As a shy, friendless kid, Molly had no trouble agreeing to the pact.

But days like these—or even the last few months—Molly had difficulties spending time with Gemma and her new fiancé. Who would have thought Gemma and Molly's brother, Sean, would have ever gotten together, never mind engaged and on the cusp of marriage? Their romance and approaching wedding triggered all the things Molly had stumped down for years, causing it to bubble to the surface. *Not in a good way.*

Molly shook her head just as a slight breeze picked up tendrils of her hair falling from her messy bun.

Gemma leaned over and tucked the red strands behind Molly's ear. "I know, it's weird. Sean and me? Us? Opposites? Who would have ever imagined it? Least of all me." She chuckled. "So, you'll be my maid of honor?"

It shouldn't have come as such a complete shock. But it was. Molly's insides knotted in a tight ball. "Ah, I'll be taking the pictures…" How could she get out of it? The last time she put on something remotely connected to a formal ceremony was her very own gorgeous wedding dress—a last fitting eight days before her own nuptials. Only they never happened.

"You can do both, up to a point, Moll." She let out a pent-up breath. "You're hiding behind your camera. Again."

"Don't you mean always?" It had been her protector and shield through her youngest years and more so now. She forced a grin. "It works."

"Not so much, friend."

"Spoilsport."

Gemma smiled. "See, like that. I miss that Molly."

There was an unmistakable catch in her friend's voice. Molly glanced over and met Gemma's concerned stare. "Me, too." She let out a painful, shivery breath. Molly jerked her gaze away and settled on the calmness of the water in front of her.

"Hey, Sean's waiting for me back at Cuppa Joe." Gemma hopped down and brushed off the back of her jeans. "Wanna join us?"

"And be a third wheel?" Again. Since they'd become a couple, Molly stopped pestering Gemma or Sean to meet up with her for dinner or a movie night or just hang out at her over the garage apartment.

"Okay, we'll find you someone." Gemma snatched up the nearby umbrella, snapped it closed, and handed it over.

"No way. Look at what you found." She chuckled when Gemma nudged her arm as she tucked the tripod under hers.

"Hey, that's my boyfriend you're talking about."

"He'd say the same about me, his sister." Deep down, Molly was truly happy for her brother and her bestie. In a strange way, they made it work, even if it had started out with them reluctantly working together on the Dear Cupid column for their hometown newspaper.

"Come on." Gemma tugged Molly's jean jacket sleeve.

Once she jumped to the ground, Molly hooked her arm through her friend's as they slowly walked to the rest of her gear. She hiked the heavy bag over her shoulder and then continued up the slight hill.

"So, what are you interested in?"

"No coffee for me. I've got an appointment soon. The rambunctious little Henderson girls. Do you think I'll even get one to pose, never mind all three?" She dragged her feet in the dew-covered grass, searching for a way to get the wiggly triplets to settle down for a few clicks of her camera.

"Work?" Gemma groaned. "Do you like them tall, lean, short, muscular…"

"Are those new code words for java nowadays? I must be so out of the loop." She'd sworn off caffeinated brews for months now. Maybe she should take it up again to deal with the upcoming trio.

"Men, Molly. I'm talking about guys. What type do you like now?"

"Gemma Valentine, you need a checkup from the neck up if you think I'm shopping for a…man." This was bad, very bad. If word got out, her friend's infamous family, especially her grams, would hunt down one, slay him, and drag him back for Molly. After all, with a last name of Valentine, they really took this love ritual seriously. And in a town called Cupid's Corner…

"We want you happy." Gemma crested the hill and halted on the sidewalk.

"I am. And who is this *we*?" Her chest tightened, waiting for the answer, facing her friend.

"Sean and me. Your folks are due back from their sabbatical trip in less than three weeks. They'll worry, too."

"Don't. I'm good. More than good." Try telling that to her parents, who never quite recovered from nearly losing her as a preemie. Her folks meant well, but they somehow assumed she remained the delicate bundle and in need of their ongoing assistance, advice, and direction in life. *That would be a no.*

"Liar. You haven't been good for a long time."

This was a new side to Gemma she'd never seen before. "Ninety percent of the time I am. It's just the romance stuff… My brother put you up to this."

She shrugged. "It came up once or a dozen times."

Molly swallowed hard. "Look, Gem. I tried dating. It was awkward and uncomfortable and confusing." All she'd done was compared him to her first and only love, Adam.

Just thinking his name sent a dart of aching through her.

How could she even think of loving someone else after him? Love meant having her heart torn out. *Been there. Done that. Not repeating. Ever.*

"You gave up too soon."

"This from the once staunch opposer of the Valentine curse, or blessing, whichever one you choose at the time."

"I was wrong, okay?"

Molly slammed a hand to her chest. "You? No. Can't be." Then she giggled as Gemma shoved her arm.

"Shut up." But her cheeks did turn pink. "I finally saw Sean for who he really is and, I don't know, fell hard for him. Gosh, after all these years, who knew?"

There was the slight tightening again in Molly's belly. "I'm happy for you two." She let out a shaky breath. "I'll be your maid of honor, all right? I'd never live it down if I didn't." Really, she wanted to celebrate their happiness, even if it was at the expense of hers. But she'd steel herself, preparing at each stage. "Only for you, friend. And my annoying older brother."

"Yeah!" Gemma side hugged her as they made their way to Cuppa Joe. "We're going to set a date today. After all the harping from my family, don't you think it's about time?"

The viselike sensation wrapped around Molly's throat again. "It's not like he's going to bolt or anything."

Gemma stilled, searching her features.

But Molly looked slightly off and over her friend's right shoulder to the big glass window of the coffee shop.

"Moll, I hate that Adam did this to you back then."

"That makes two of us, pal." She caught the movement at the table behind the glass. Molly waved to her brother. "Your heartthrob is coming. That's my cue to skedaddle. You two have fun. See you soon." She hugged Gemma. Gratitude rushed through her at her friend's comforting embrace.

"Call me later. Promise. Wait, we'll do dinner instead. Tonight at the new Martinelli's place."

"Maybe." Molly checked Main Street traffic in both directions and hustled across the road, her gear bouncing and banging against her sides. *More bruises to follow.* At the corner of Vine, she turned to look back. Sean had joined Gemma, placing his arm around her. Even from here their newfound love shone.

A lance of sheer, undeniable envy shot through Molly. "Don't move!" She picked up her camera from where it hung around her neck and took several shots. "Got it!"

They chuckled at her and shook their heads.

She turned away then, unable to bear anymore lovey-dovey, mushy stuff for one morning. Geez, one would think a photographer who needed the business to stay afloat would make peace with this wedding nonsense once and for all.

The popular wedding season was right around the corner. Since the big Valentine's Day festivities in town six weeks ago, Cupid's Corner developed more and more interest for the summer nuptials. She'd had nearly twenty requests so far. That was some heavy-duty chunk of change she sneered at—or ran away from.

She couldn't afford to anymore.

Molly marched down Vine Street, gazing straight ahead as she passed by her fellow neighbor businesses. Yeah, that flower shop right next door with sample bouquets was a tough one to avoid. But avoid she did.

When she reached her shop, she hesitated with the key. Looking up and around, the enormity of her opening her own place, Moment in Time, hit her hard. The painted white trim outlined the poster-like family photos displayed in the two big windows. She smiled at her friends and neighbors in those pictures, each one a piece of her life. And she'd given them a lifetime memory to hold on to—even if they were tried and true poses.

That mattered, didn't it?

Forget her teenage dreams of traveling the world as a re-nowned international, award-winning photographer. That and having Gemma as her journalist sidekick. This place came to fruition because of her love of photography, captur-ing a moment in time forever.

So what if she had to compromise to keep it going? She preferred landscapes and buildings—the lush beauty and then smooth curves and sharp angles. Yeah, that last one, blame it on her brother the architect. Places over people. One didn't necessarily negate the other altogether—however, her priority had shifted to the reality of her situation. Her bread and butter came from people's milestone events, celebrated with joy and happy tears.

Funny when she wasn't great with people. Now places and things—that didn't talk back or squirm or refuse to comply—they were her safe, comfort zone. Too bad no one paid for those landscapes or building shots, not in a small hometown like hers.

She let out a shaky breath, knowing what she had to do.

Take that giant leap off the cliff and into full-on fear mode or sink to the dark, bottomless pit and wallow in a wasteland of a regular, boring job.

Maybe after ten years and ten thousand weddings she could switch to something that brought passion to her again. In the meantime, she could still take excursions and document her beauties on the side.

Her hand shook as she braced her heart to the inevitable pain of what was to come.

Time to book the late May and June weddings.

Recovering hopeless romantic, my butt.

Chapter Two

ADAM LARSON ABSENTLY closed the door of his white company pickup truck with the bold green logo—Elite Renovations—on the side. The definite metal click echoed in the early morning stillness.

"Everything's changed and nothing has changed." His words sliced through the silence, awakening a flock of black crows in the nearby tree—their wings fluttering and carrying them away from one of the heavily leaved red maples.

He followed their flight, a perfect arrow formation as the leader guided them to the crest of the half-ruined barn. They perched there, expectant.

With a sharp tug behind his ribs, Adam sucked in a shallow, painful breath.

The hundred-year-old structure—worn wood exterior with most of the roof line intact—thrust him back into his past.

Playing here, working summers stacking hay bales in that barn, kissing pretty girls in the loft, sitting up there in the second story as he looked out over the pond behind it, and dreaming of his future of playing professional football. Each incredible moment came swift and crystal-clear.

"Molly." He nearly ripped her name from his suddenly tight chest. She'd been there holding his big hand in her tiny one, hoping right along with him, since sophomore year in high school.

Only none of their dreams had come true.

Because of him.

Leaving her meant cutting out a part of himself. But he'd had to…

Now, Adam shook his head and slowly moved around the front of his truck and through the packed hard dirt that forged a path and patches of brown grass for nearly a half mile from the end of the overgrown driveway and back into the once thriving land. The scrunch of dead leaves and small limbs snapping under his booted feet echoed in his ears.

"'Bout time you showed up." Mr. Owen Pickens scratched his gray-bearded chin and lifted a thick, bushy eyebrow as he walked toward him from the back of the once grand Victorian house, now dull and dingy and in need of repair. "Thought you might chicken out, son."

Adam smiled at the old farmer and moved closer to shake his callused hand. Even at this very moment, Adam wondered if he'd done the right thing by buying the place— farm, house, barn, land, and everything on the vast, dilapidated property.

It was either the development company plowing it down to build seventy or more houses or Adam. Once he discovered his former boss's dilemma in being forced to sell, Adam stepped in to purchase it instead. Two choices. Pickens chose

Adam. "Me? I never met a challenge I didn't like." Until this moment.

"True. In your younger days, we had quite the time keeping you in one piece most summers."

"You, my mom, and my dad." His folks and Adam were part-time farmhands during planting and harvest seasons. A swirl of funny and daring escapades rushed through Adam's mind. His smile came easy.

"Yep, those were the days."

Many of the good times centered around this place for him. At least the long hours of work kept him outdoors in the warm sunshine, breathing fresh country air, and not cooped up. "Coming here after football games. Bonfires. Fishing down at the pond."

"Fish aren't as good as they used to be, but I still throw a line every Sunday after church."

"And your boat?" He couldn't stop the fondness from entering his voice.

"Patch her up every time she springs a leak. She's better than any new metal ones from a store. Those are for the fancy-schmancy rentals. You know, that risk factor and insurance."

Adam recalled taking Molly out on the prized dingy the first time as she clung to the sides, her fingers turning white. Funny, she wasn't at all concerned when she picked up her ever-present, faithful camera and started clicking away.

No, but he had been when she stood up and over-reached. He'd had to catch her from falling over. She'd plunked down on the wooden seat, her face glowing, her silky red hair in disarray, and her striking blue eyes sparkling at the images she'd gotten.

Molly.

Her incredible smile!

Another ache.

"You know, most times it seemed like summer camp." The majority of Adam's adventures, he'd fared well. Not so much two or three. Either giving or receiving.

Yeah, like that one time, a week before his wedding, he stared at the woman who owned his heart and had to tell her he couldn't go through with it. Too bad he'd never finished what he'd been too ashamed to say to Molly.

Regret and guilt warred in him until this very day.

The undeniable surging feelings had been the deciding factor in buying a place in Cupid's Corner. Making things right with Molly—and the town he'd grown to love after his family moved there when he was in junior high—seemed important. All that had happened from the comfortable distance of his company office over a hundred miles away and weeks ago—finding the article online about the declining farm in dire straits and on the sales block.

Now that he was here, the memories and emotions flooded back and clouded his usually clear thinking.

Molly.

What would she look like now? Searching online, he couldn't find anything about her marrying. So incredibly sad when she dreamed about it—all the little details that went into the ceremony and reception—and their lives together after. He'd yanked that all away from her. What would she be like now? Six years changed a person—his high school sweetheart. And she deserved to love and be loved.

Adam tamped down on the bitterness flooding him. Jealousy, too.

But he'd given up that right to have a say in her life and a place in her heart. And he'd paid dearly for it ever since.

"Been following you through the years, son. Your mom's been writing Christmas cards for her and your dad from Florida and keeping me posted. You did good. Even bought them a nice place. Construction jobs to fixing houses to remodeling and on to owning your own company. Not many people would have seen that in you back then. But I did. Oh, you might seem all laidback and fun-loving, but you had that drive. No doubt about it. And coming from the wrong side of the tracks and everything. Something about proving people wrong, I guess."

Ignoring the mention of his sore, prickly past, Adam tilted his head to the barn. "I'm surprised you're giving it up, Mr. Pickens. But I'm glad you settled on me to buy it."

He walked slower, strolling beside the former owner, assessing the property closely—several structures, tree lines, picturing the intensive work to not only get the barn in tip-top shape for the upcoming events but the grounds as well. He'd leave the large, white Victorian main house for later. Adam had two months to pull this off. Close and unforgivable deadlines were his forte. But on something so important? Now, that would have to be seen to be believed.

"Once you saw the article in the paper after that last storm came through, well, you gave me an offer I couldn't refuse. Lifelong resident caretaker. Now, that's something I'd never shake a stick at." Pickens marveled as he looked lovingly around the overgrown brushes and trees, weathered buildings, and unkempt grounds of his former family homestead.

Grinning at the old familiar phrase, Adam turned to the older man. "Who better than you? And we'll keep your family name on it in some way. Seems only right, don't you think?"

"Wedding venue?" The older man's voice croaked. "Never imagined that."

"What better opportunity for one than in Cupid's Corner? It's practically considered the love destination in New England for Valentine's Day. Hopefully, with expanding into weddings and by the time we get the word out, in the country, too." Adam's mind immediately went to Molly. If it hadn't been for her photographs—in the local paper he still subscribed to online—of the before and after shots of the damaged barn weeks ago, Adam would never have contacted Pickens, put a bid in, much less come back here.

But that tug drew him in. Awareness. Curiosity. Longing to know if she'd ever moved on and he hadn't crushed her soul completely. She still went by Molly McCleary in the photo credits, so he'd wondered until it burned in him.

Had she ever forgiven him?

An icy stone of apprehension sat hard in his gut.

Dismissing it, or at least trying to, Adam sprinted into action. He made a half dozen calls—his ever-efficient executive assistant, his best foreman, the landscapers, the lumber company on his speed-dial, the hardware store, and then his real estate guy to push for the known permits now and the upcoming ones to follow.

All the while, he relied on Pickens's handy information given for access roads, any foreseen bumps with getting heavy-duty equipment in, and simple hand-drawn maps of the area and property on Adam's legal pad to orient him and his people of the myriad of things left out of the blueprints.

"Looks like we're hopping already." Pickens rubbed his hands together. "Haven't been this excited in I don't know when." He shook his head. "You know, I wasn't too sure about this. But I couldn't keep the place up anymore. No family left to speak of and all. Business in my kind of farming is slow these days. Well, I'm about fifteen years on the other side of my game, if you know what I mean."

Adam patted him on the shoulder. "I hear you." Change was hard on someone like this guy. He'd come from generations of farmers. It was in his family's blood. To be the last one and only sixty-five or so, although the gray hair did age him more, without any kids to take over, Pickens had hung on a decade too long. "Glad you're on board. You're a big help already."

"Good to know this old dog hasn't had his last day yet."

"Let's go over the immediate plans, so you'll be able to direct my people when they land in a day or two."

"Me?"

"You're my right-hand man on this project. Your knowledge and expertise will be invaluable. You know the town, the people, the land, the farm, what would work, what wouldn't… Pretty much my eyes and ears."

"Sounds like you won't be here."

"No mistake, my friend. I'll be here, every step of the way, working hard." He couldn't afford not to; he'd staked his business on this venture. He'd plunked down a sizable chunk of change and gave up lucrative contracts for months to come to devote his time and effort to making this a success. All in. Including him.

His instinct knew a good thing when it felt it—his gut, too.

Adam had scraped by in the beginning until he'd realized working for himself could get him a lot further in a shorter amount of time and then he'd built up a thriving business.

Now, deep inside, he sensed this was riskier than the other ones.

This wasn't only his company's livelihood on the line. It was Adam's reputation in Cupid's Corner, his adopted hometown, and the people who lived there.

He had so much to make up for and to prove once and for all.

Can I rise up to the challenge of being a force to be reckoned with in this small town? Or will they judge me for leaving everything and them behind, especially their sweet girl next door Molly? Will my past still color my future?

Nearly a half hour later of exploring and mentally and physically making notes about what had to be accomplished and in what priority, Adam sliced a hand through his hair, wondering how he was going to move mountains to get this wedding enterprise up and running in two short months and then leave it in the capable hands of someone he had to hire to run the entire operation. Until then, it was on his shoulders to create a miracle…

Yeah, especially since the only person he wanted to and knew could pull this off with him was the very same woman he'd left nearly six years ago in this exact spot.

Damn it, he'd done the unthinkable and now he needed to make amends—big ones by offering her a part of one of her long ago, starry-eyed dreams after they became engaged, of being knee-deep in documenting happy, loving couples joining together on their special day and Adam hoping for even an ounce of redemption in her eyes.

His beautiful, hopeless romantic…

Chapter Three

M OLLY SCURRIED AROUND her nearly pristine shop—
old hardwood flooring, a long counter on one end
with a register, her desk, and computer just behind it with
lots of white shelves and cubbies with related items for sale
decorating them, a white painted round table with comfy
chairs under one window, and the blocked-off back area of
her studio—trying to tie up loose ends before the triplets and
their mom arrived. Thankfully, she'd set up the shoot last
night before she left.

Floor-to-ceiling white cotton fabric hung by clamps from
the rod she'd had installed. Her stands with black shade
umbrellas and adjustable lights were in position. Her trusty
tripod stood ready. Stools at varying heights waited, even one
behind her for their mom to appease them.

"All set. With a half hour to spare."

In the meantime, she had phone messages to listen to, jot
down, and make notes to return calls.

Half of the dozen were about weddings.

She gritted her teeth.

Later, she'd sit down and calculate the prices and figure

out just how many she really had to commit herself to. Of course, she was giving a freebie to her brother and her future sister-in-law.

The Valentine's Day weddings over six weeks ago hadn't been as traumatic or stressful in the end—all based at the town square and in the gazebo. She'd blocked out the more sappy ones and pretended she was filming a movie shoot— they weren't real, just actors playing a part. She'd had Gemma pitching in between her duties and all were simple, outside ones near the festivities.

"Easy-peasy."

Now the traditional church ones with full-on receptions? Yeah, not so excited about those. They'd hit too close to her own doomed one nearly six years ago.

Brushing by a stack of mail on the edge of the counter, she dislodged it. Envelopes and postcards fell like confetti to the floor.

"Just my luck." She scrambled to snatch them up.

Some she recognized as junk mail, the five predictable weekly colorful postcards from her parents surely with loving, gentle nudges on eating more veggies or getting more rest or instructions on when to take her vitamins and which ones to add for the season, some were bills—they were mounting against her—and a few unrecognizable ones drew her curiosity.

There was something about these—all from the same Elite Renovations company—that piqued her interest. Again. She'd ignored their emails in spam and then deleted them. But then the letters came. She'd let them pile up the last few busy days jam-packed with prom requests, graduate shoots, and Kyle and Kyra's multi-appointments at different hours of the day for their engagement pics.

"What would a construction company be writing to me about? Four letters. Hello, I've already done a remodel on my new place. I'm not going to hire you."

She went to toss them in the trash, but something held her back. A little blip of guilt urged her to be the professional businesswoman she claimed she needed to be in order to get this place out of the red and fast. May's rent wasn't going to pay itself. Or the utility bills.

"Grow up, Moll, already. You can't rely on your family and friends to hold you up forever, now can you? And you've got to convince Mom and Dad you're capable of running a business and your life when they swing back in town in less than three weeks."

Pep talk?

"Sure. More like scared straight."

Blowing out a breath, she ripped open the earliest post-marked letter. Her frown increased. "Interested in employing you…"

She cleared her throat. "For what exactly?" The name of the company didn't ring a bell. She looked closer and realized it was headquartered over a hundred miles away.

Going through each one, her curiosity grew. "A new job in the area? Documenting a rebuild?" The last one, dated two days ago, rattled her the most. Her legs wobbled and she reached for a stool—dropping into it. As she tried to steady her shaking hands, numbness invaded her, leaving her icy-cold on the outside and trembling in her belly on the inside.

"The old Pickens place… They're renovating the barn? Into a wedding venue?" She pressed the letter to her chest and with her eyes squeezed tightly, a hot tear slipped out and streaked down her cheek.

The special place on the hill overlooking the pond had been in the newspaper lately, along with the photos she'd taken of the beloved spot, with the terrible storm damage, making it unusable. There was talk of destroying it all together and a development company, putting up row after row of houses outside of town, wanted the prime Pickens location for more of the same.

But here was hope. Only it involved the *W* word again.

And this renovation company wanted to hire her? Smack dab there where…

"Mine. My dream wedding…right there years ago. Well, almost." Only the groom dumped her a week before, crushing her heart.

Her glance caught the neatly stacked growing pile of postcards from her parents—all added up to their months of contact, aside from the flurry of emails every time they landed in a town with internet, regarding their concern for her and her ability to care for and support herself.

Molly brushed aside the ribbon of doubt each one stirred. Again.

"Get over yourself, Moll. Time for your big girl panties. This is business 101. It's a paying job. Do not let your emotions get in the way." She blew out a breath. "I got this, right?" She shifted her shoulders back, shrugged, and then shoved down the enormity of it, burying it.

I am not a wuss. I am not a wuss. I can do this. Just blank out the W stuff like I did before. It's all pretend. Everyone's dressed up in costumes in a movie and there's a pretty cake…

MOLLY FUMBLED THROUGH the session, trying to focus on the three adorable, brown-haired little girls. Their harried mother—a grown-up version of the cuties—coaxed at first, then ordered, and then finally pleaded for the girls' cooperation.

None worked.

She'd gotten a few shots, but when Molly checked not all of the kiddos were looking at the camera at the same time. She never photoshopped or cut and pasted, but this one may be her undoing.

It was nerves.

With ten minutes to spare after falling apart—yeah, that happened—when she read the letter, Molly had dashed away the tears, looked in her handy mirror and blinked rapidly to clear her blue eyes of any telltale signs, swept up her long red hair in a high ponytail, and then chugged a half bottle of cool water.

So, outwardly, she looked the part. Inwardly, she was a big tangle of a hot mess.

"Girls! Girls, stop!" Their mother nearly wept with frustration. "I'm sorry about this. It's been so hard. My husband is out of town on business. I've never had them this long on my own. I swear they do this on purpose."

"We'll reschedule." Molly gulped, knowing she could use the deposit for her light bill due in two days. Gone. *Now what do I do?*

"Oh, could you? That would be so helpful." The gleam of desperation and a ray of hope leapt in Robin Henderson's pretty eyes.

The woman's phone rang, startling her.

She fished it out of her back pocket like it was a lifeline. "Oh, I have to get this. It's the Realtor. We put a bid in for a new house. With three two-year-olds…"

"Go ahead."

"Could you watch them?" She didn't even wait for a proper response from Molly. However, she answered the cell phone, nodded twice, and then marched to the door, barging out onto the sidewalk.

What just happened here? Molly looked at the squirming trio, pushy and giggly, and running after each other.

"Hey! Guys, uh, girls!" Molly's voice failed her.

She'd never really babysat before and wasn't at all confident around little ones this age. She'd tackled schoolkids with wit and empathy for ages. But that had taken a great deal of effort on her part. And usually a teacher or someone from the school admin staff oversaw the children, making sure they behaved.

The one thing Molly did know was most kids—even adults for that matter—did not like getting their pictures taken. So she had to make it fun.

"Dress-up time!"

Three little darlings halted, their long brown ringlets bouncing, their peachy-pink cheeks brighter, and their blue eyes wide and glowing.

"I wanna be a cowgirl." The middle one, Jules, stepped closer and off the staged area.

"Me a princess soccer player." Desie came forward.

"Both?" Molly grinned, surprised she'd captured their interest and by their imaginations.

"Uh-huh." She gave a curt nod, springy curls dancing.

The last one, Vivie, stuck her hands on her hips. "Ballerina basketball champ."

"That's a tall order." Molly's mind raced as she shoved herself to her feet. "Come on, let's see what we have back here." She'd tucked away most of the costume stuff from Gemma's family's now-closed antiques store, thinking she might need it someday.

Well, I guess someday is today.

She dragged out five bulky boxes from her storage area and the girls squealed with delight, yanking out hats, shoes, trophies, tulle and tutus, and fluff and fabric of some or other scarf or dress and dumping them all over the floor.

Scattered items spread far and wide. The girls giggled as they plucked out what they wanted and chased others as they rolled away, rushing to catch them.

In less than ten minutes, with their mom pacing up and down the sidewalk still on the phone in what looked like a heated debate, Molly helped the little girls with their outfits. Next, she dropped the white backdrop and revealed a light charcoal gray one hanging behind it.

Molly scrambled for her camera and began taking shots, first of them discovering the goodies, trying on different ones, and then as they found their favorites and sat—under Molly's direction—for fun and silly photos.

Her heart leapt. Excitement grew.

She loved these shots, so enamored of the glee on the triplets' faces. Now, they were helping each other, posing them or handing over a baseball cap and bat for Jules.

"This one, Desie."

Losing track of time, Molly didn't stop snapping pictures until the door flew open.

"What's going on here?" Robin Henderson's exasperated voice rang through the room.

The girls jumped to attention, guilty looks on their faces.

"Oh, no, it's me, Mrs. H. The girls were a ball of energy. I thought they'd want to play." Molly stood up to face her. "I hope that's okay. We were having lots of fun."

Relief washed over the young mother's expression. "Most days I'm at my wit's end."

"Times three." Molly grinned. "I understand. Look, do you mind if I print some of these? I think they'd be really cute for their grandmothers. For Mother's Day gifts. It's only a few weeks away."

"Why not? I won't have the time to shop for anything else anyway." Her shoulders sagged. "We're counteroffering on the house. Hopefully, we'll get it and be able to spread out a little more. We'll even have a dedicated playroom for the girls."

A few years older than Molly, the mother appeared to be

doing a great job in raising her surprise triplets. The dad spent more time working two jobs to make up for the loss of income.

Molly swallowed hard, wondering if that would have been an image of herself and Adam...

Why did he keep invading her thoughts?

Weddings and babies.

Yeah, no.

With a great deal of effort, Molly firmly stuck her business back in the forefront of her mind.

She had no time to waste with thoughts of what could have been. Adam left her behind and set out on a new life.

I don't even want to know if he replaced me, if he's married and has kids...

Her heart hitched, and she ignored it.

Time to put the past behind and move ahead.

Maybe the first step was facing her demons. After getting the deposit for the sitting and seeing the exuberant little family off, Molly grabbed the letter stuffed in her back pocket and reread the information, hardening her resolve.

"Okay, Pickens Farms, you and I are going to face off and today I make my peace with you once and for all." *Oh yeah, former hopeless romantic scores a point or a dozen.*

A thought slipped into the back of her mind, making her shiver.

For better or worse.

Chapter Four

WITH A WHITE hardhat on his head, Adam surveyed the damaged structure; age and recent fierce winds had toppled the heavy rooster weathervane. Thankfully, the caved-in area hadn't brought down the rest of the old barn.

How the weight hadn't dragged down more portions, like a domino effect, he had no idea. The solid wood beams were sturdier than any modern day substitution. The floor below showed the massive water damage from that storm and more rain.

The work that needed to be done piled up in Adam's mind, more than he'd factored in after the inspection report landed in his email inbox. *Wishful thinking it wasn't so bad or blatant disregard because he was going to do it anyway?* He noted the foundation issues, sagging rafters—that he now walked along—and more gaps in this side of the roof, allowing the afternoon sun to spill through like little halos.

Surefooted, he walked along the chunky, aged lengths like a gymnast walking a balance beam. He gained the one section of loft near the upper window and, with a great deal of muscle, slid back the cumbersome, stuck hay bale doors.

The warped wood scraped, the sound splitting the air with ear-piercing squeals.

Once open, Adam stilled at the magnificent sight. He'd guaranteed this was the best view in Cupid's Corner, bar none—the slope of the grassy land dipped to meet the calm, peaceful pond, Pickens's battered boat tied with the thick rope to the small dock, the four metal ones turned over in a neat line nearby on the green grass, the new bridge, and beyond the overgrown limbs of trees the outline of the many familiar buildings in town.

Memories slammed into him of being here in the hot summer days and longing rose up in him. He'd been on the outside looking in. If only he could have felt a part of it, a part of the Cupid's Corner family.

That wasn't a given for a kid from the wrong side of the tracks, even if he did everything to erase that image—then and now.

With a great deal of effort, he tugged his gaze away and forced himself to look at the solid wood frame. His breath shivered out of him when he saw it—the heart he'd carved with his and Molly's initials inside. That was his way to get up the nerve to ask her to marry him.

For some unknown reason, she'd said yes...

A car engine coming up the drive grabbed his attention. His guys couldn't have packed up and made it so quick, could they?

By the time he zigzagged his steps across the few sturdy boards remaining, a lone car door slammed shut and foot-steps stirred up what was left of the loose gravel on the ground.

The ladder had listed to the side, so he crammed on his work gloves, reached down, and then grabbed tight to a rafter.

Just like old times…

AFTER ONE THAT afternoon, Molly poked her head into the barn—careful of spiderwebs and creepy crawlies. For good measure, she lifted her camera and took a few shots at the shadowy insides interspersed with rays of light from the hole-filled roof.

A rush of mixed memories and images from back then piled on. *Waiting here for Adam to finish working. The scent of fresh hay filling her senses, the warmth of sunshine on her face as she peeked out the second-story hay door, and the heady anticipation building inside her at the promise of seeing him.* Even now, the sweet tug drew her farther inside.

Her interest piqued, wanting to explore more and find little treasures of images for photos—an old farm implement here or an iron-forged piece of fence for the main house there.

"Should have changed clothes." Her whispered words dropped into the hush of silence.

The empty company truck was outside. Mr. Pickens wasn't in sight. So where was everyone?

With more guts than glory, Molly entered through the ten-foot-high barn door opening, blinking to grow accustomed to the dimmer light inside.

Suddenly, she noted a swift movement from above, descending, and then swinging from a beam toward her. A man dropped down less than ten feet away—his boots thwacking against the hard-packed dirt—holding his balance and then rising slowly.

She squeaked, backing up. But not before the past clashed with the present. "Adam!"

Her blood rushed to her head like shards of stabbing glass and then to her chest, spreading ice in her veins. Within seconds, it switched gears, warming to creep up her neck and into her cheeks.

All the while, air from her lungs ballooned and rose but remained trapped in her parched throat.

"Moll?" Adam shook his head, removing his white hardhat. He blinked and she swore he lost color. "I never thought you'd show…"

Stunned wonder would be the last thing she'd expect from Adam. Gosh, did she just say his name in her head? Or maybe she'd imagined him after thinking of him earlier. It had been so very long since she allowed herself to fully, completely dream about him, never mind look at him—or the many pictures she'd taken of him.

She assessed him, quickly and thoroughly, as she would a person to photograph. Her body hummed and she berated herself for liking his tall, leaner frame. He still had muscles, more taut and defined than in his high school football playing days.

Molly swallowed hard and focused on his beautiful face.

His dark blond hair was shorter, making the angles and planes of his features stand out even more in sharp comparison to the boy he'd been. But his eyes—greener now, somehow—never broke contact from her own.

Then she repeated his words in her head. "Wait. You never thought I'd show." Realization dropped into every fiber of her being. "Y-you." She lifted her hand and stuck her thumb over her shoulder. "*That* Elite Renovations." It wasn't a question. Light bulbs and bells went off in her head. He wanted to hire her for this renovation.

"Still so very smart." He strolled to her, brushing a hand through his hair, ruffling it. On him, it just looked hotter. The muscle in his jaw jumped the closer he approached.

A yard away, he halted, drinking her in—or so it felt down to her bones.

Emotions chased across his eyes, darkening them. "Gorgeous."

Molly gasped, intrigued at the shift and fighting the sharp tug of awareness. This wasn't like it was supposed to be. It hadn't been back then. The high school dreamy state of wanting him had altered drastically, replaced by this undeniable heat shivering through her. Why now? *Yeah, this isn't happening. Not on my watch. Minus a point for even thinking this. Some recovering hopeless romantic I am.* "Is that all you have to say for yourself, Adam Larson?"

"I'm sorry I hurt you."

The four simple words—ones he'd given before—were softer, yet stronger than anything she'd experienced from him in the past. They rang true, shaking her.

"I've heard that before." She nearly choked out the whispered words, trying to hold herself from crumbling apart right in front of him.

"They were true then and they're truer now."

Heartfelt. Somehow she did understand that part. Still, there were so many unanswered questions. But she was done trying to make sense of it; she'd needed to let it go, as her friends and family continually urged her to do.

"We good? Works for me. I'll see you around. Or not." Molly turned on her heel and marched out—her heavy camera and its strap yanking on her neck—trembling uncontrollably.

Never in her wildest imagination did she ever think Adam would return to Cupid's Corner. He didn't lie. And he'd told her point blank he was done with the small town and everyone else in it when he shattered her heart six years ago.

"Aren't you even curious? Not one bit?"

His voice was closer than she expected, making her jump.

She twirled around, clamping a hand on her swinging camera. "About you?"

"The job. Should I start with the deposit?" He named a mid, four-figure amount. "You get that today."

Gulping hard, she steeled herself, hoping her eyes weren't bugging out right about now. "That's—"

"Not enough?" He shrugged. "I'll double it."

Okay, heart, don't lurch like that ever again. That would pay for months of rent and expenses.

Frowning, Molly eyed him and then let her gaze travel to

his company truck and then back again. "Done well for yourself?" She couldn't quite bring herself to say his name again.

It felt too intimate.

"Fair enough." He shoved his hands in his pockets and rocked on his heels. "For a guy without a college education."

The way he avoided her stare made her aware he knew more about her business than she did about his. When he couldn't afford to further his schooling, she'd done so and look where they were now. Completely in opposite positions apparently.

"You think you have me pegged, don't you?" Anger stirred low in her belly. Her pride bristled.

Adam gave her that look—the half scowl, half smile she'd adored in school. And it sent her pulse off like a hammer in the spot low on her neck.

His eyes found it and held steady. "You help me. I'll help you."

"That's it?" No strings attached?

He jerked his stare to her eyes and captured them.

There was something simmering below the surface she couldn't read, but made her highly conscious of him and her own responses to him. Yeah, that little flutter inside.

"I need you, Moll." His words came out soft yet urgent.

They tugged at her. She fought hard. "I..." She swallowed hard. "Don't need you."

His features hardened. "Duly noted. But this is business. Full access to document the renovation of Cupid's Corner beloved landmark to a unique and fascinating wedding venue and events center overlooking the picturesque town pond. A close-up, once-in-a-lifetime chance for both of…our businesses. More publicity than we will ever get individually." Right before her eyes, she noted a brighter gleam come into his.

Adam shrugged while he rubbed the back of his neck. "We could always push it and go for a, uh, fake reunion."

Her heart rate *thug-thugged* in her chest. Their past involvement would play right into the hands of the local gossips and rumor mill. What better way to market a wedding venture than to bring together Cupid's Corner's very own high school sweethearts for a second chance romance?

Oh, he was very good.

"Forget about doubling, I'll give you five times the amount. Do you want it or not?"

Five, did he say *five*? That would ensure another year or two. And she could pick and choose the jobs she took. All for taking pictures of the renovation, being around the weddings—that might be a little sticky there with that love stuff—and the very high price of a pretend relationship—no, worse, *reunion* with a heaping side of speculation, curiosity, and unfounded conclusions from the townspeople, with the guy who broke her heart.

A few months of faking it. "Dang you, Adam Larson, for doing this to me." Again.

Impossible decisions. Dreams crushed. Now dangling new, exciting adventures and temptations in front of her…

The nerve of him!

Chapter Five

ADAM COULDN'T BREATHE. His lungs burned. His gaze didn't falter.

From the moment he saw her standing in the barn entrance over two hours ago he'd been out of sorts.

Not in a good way, either.

Molly McCleary had never looked so amazing to him before. She was still slim, yet curvy, if that were even possible. But under her button-down white shirt—half of it tucked in and half out—skinny, worn jeans that emphasized her perfect slightly round hips and long legs, and her dusty maroon boots, she'd become even more attractive. How was *that* possible?

A beautiful woman, who had him tripping over his thoughts and throwing everything out there to get her to agree to what exactly…? He wasn't even sure himself.

It started as a way to pay Cupid's Corner back—to lift them out of what would surely be housing congestion, clogged streets, and losing the sweet small-town feel. And a part of him admitted he *wanted* to see Molly again. Once he realized he could make the barn into a wedding venue, he knew deep in his bones he'd *needed* her for this project. Needed to give her something now when he could never do it before. But the rest? The couple thing? Not in his initial plans—nowhere near what he expected to come out of him. Not. At. All.

Her pulled-back red hair and soft tendrils framed her delicate face. Her blue, blue eyes stood out against her pale skin. But it was the look—a little miffed, yet intrigued—that had Adam's blood humming.

That had to be why he'd pivoted at the last minute and plucked the fake reunion out of the air. Otherwise, he couldn't begin to fathom why he'd made such a ridiculous offer and risk her flat-out no. But she hadn't turned him down yet…

Most considered her fragile and dainty back in the day. That preemie stigma thing stuck—her parents emphasized it often enough. He'd protected Molly then. Until he couldn't any longer.

No one was more aware of how breakable she'd seemed than Adam.

However, staying would have shattered her delicate life and her illusions into little pieces. It just would have taken a heck of a lot longer over years to see the effects wear on her.

He wasn't proud of what he'd done. Not even when he reminded himself he saved her from the hard life in store for her.

"Quit staring, Larson." She'd gritted her teeth until she snapped at him.

Stopping along the thick line of trees after half walking,

half hiking the property, she turned to him with grim lines etched on her features.

"I like the view." A little spark of admiration for her toughness went off inside him. She'd never confronted anything when he knew her.

"That's it? You want me…" She cleared her throat. "To follow the progress of the transformation of this place from farmer's barn and great hangout spot growing up to your new venture."

"*Wedding venue*, for the most part. Events center. Reunions. Parties. Holidays. You name it."

"Pictures fed to *Cupid's Corner Gazette* and more on both our websites. A video every now and then. Maybe…a coffee table book for the town."

"And sold to tourists. I read somewhere that you and Gemma's grandfather were slowly putting together a similar book on the history of Cupid's Corner."

"Keeping up with…us?" Her voice stuck and she swallowed hard. "His vast wealth of knowledge on everything, old archive photos, and my current day pictures." Her blue eyes lit from within.

It made his heart catch. "Perfect for you, Moll." Pride beamed in his chest. In spite of everything, she'd found a source of happiness.

"The project is slow going. Work does that sort of thing."

He smiled at her sharp edges. "So, this will make it easier for you."

"How so?"

"Didn't I tell you?" He'd kept it a secret. Dangling the money she needed to succeed in her business—discovered by digging online, that and her still single status—in order for her to be able to hand select her assignments while allowing him to launch his venture and silently beg for her forgiveness seemed right at the moment he thought of it weeks ago. Not so much now. "You get to be the premier, star wedding day photographer for the venue. It's in the contract."

She bristled.

His heart thumped. She loved weddings, right? At least she had.

He tried another tactic. "Moll, Cupid's Corner is a one holiday wonder so far. Once word gets out I'm creating a wedding venue—and it will—there will be plenty of other related companies trying to get in on the bandwagon and cash in on the appeal. Outsiders. Buying land and scooping up dying businesses from our neighbors, our friends. I'm not about to let them down. You, the town sweetheart, deserve this chance to be at the forefront of this, too, to help me lead the way for our...place." He nearly choked on the last; this small piece of heaven was theirs. In his heart it would always be.

Take what I'm offering you. That's all I can ever give you. Adam pressed a little harder, playing on her hot buttons. "That's if you're up to it."

"YOU'RE CONSIDERING WHAT?" Gemma stared at Molly

across the sleek restaurant table hours later. Her wide eyes nearly popped out of her head.

Molly wanted to slink down farther in her booth as the other familiar customers—many she'd known all her life—in the new Italian place in the converted old fire station jerked their heads to their table. Thank goodness Molly hadn't mentioned the fake reunion part. That would have gone over like never.

"Can you yell a little louder? I don't think Mrs. Martinelli heard it in the kitchen."

"Wait until Sean hears about this. And your folks."

Yikes. This was getting a little dicey, even for Molly. "Hold up. Do we have to tell them? I mean, they are my family. I know how I have to ease them into my way of thinking." *Like that's going to ever happen in my lifetime.* She cringed.

"Do you really think you'll bring them around in say, ten years? Yeah, that's not happening, friend. He hurt you. You're still damaged and broken."

The words struck Molly right in her chest, hard and fast. "Ow, that smarts."

"Seriously? Don't think you're fooling us for one second—"

"What's she fooling us about now?" Sean joined them, coming up swiftly behind Molly, giving her a brief hug and then going to Gemma's side of the booth. He slid in and along the red bench seat and then leaned over and kissed her cheek. "Hey, missed you."

"Me, too."

"I think I'm traumatized every time I see that. Oh, my eyes!" Molly tried to lighten up the conversation.

Still, a ton of dread sat in her gut—not conducive to sharing a meal with them or anytime soon.

Her brother sat back and eyed her. "I know you two have this weird shorthand language that's nearly indecipherable, so can you go back and start over in plain English for me?"

Molly waved a hand in dismissal. "Really, it's nothing." She shot Gemma a fierce look.

"Nothing as in teaming up with her ex—"

"Some friend you are." Molly gritted her teeth and fiddled with her straw, dipping it up and down and clinking ice cubes in her nearly full strawberry lemonade.

"Whoa now! Ex as in Adam? He's back in Cupid's Corner?" Sean sat up straight, jerking his gaze from her to Gemma and back to her again. "Moll?"

She groaned. "It's not like I knew or anything. He owns a construction company and took on renovating old man Pickens's barn for a…um, you know, place."

"Make that a *wedding* venue." Gemma nudged Sean with an elbow. "Our hopeless romantic here—"

"I'm in recovery. Remember?" *How many points am I down now?*

"Let's count the double feature rom com nights you've dragged me to in the past, what, nearly six years? Nope, make that an even ten, since high school." Gemma's stern look spoke volumes.

Molly slid down in her seat, dodging the curious looks from nearby diners. *Pull your chair a little closer, why don't you?* "Those? Just a strange—"

"Obsession."

"No. No, I've been doing better." She shrugged. "Since Valentine's Day. You two have that one cornered."

That was her awakening moment. She'd never have anything compared to their happiness, not even close. Molly didn't expect lightning to strike her twice in one lifetime.

The ring of the bell over the door dinged, almost like background noise. However, the silence that followed and the stares directed behind Molly focused on the newcomer and the pique of unusual interest in said person.

A thump of sickening dread pumped into her chest, over and over again. *He didn't just do what I think he did, did he?*

"Adam." Sean stood.

Yep, he had come to a public place where I am. Molly's insides knotted.

"Sean. Good to see you."

"I can't say the same, bud." Her brother's voice warred between standing up for her and seeing his old football teammate—the star running back.

As if time had slowed to a standstill, Molly sensed the building tension all around. She scanned the nearly full tables, recognizing the deeply concerned looks on her neighbors and Cupid's Corner's families. Somehow it clicked.

While they backed her, they objected to Adam's presence here, maybe even in town. That wasn't fair. Then or now.

He'd never done anything directly to them—only to her.

She jerked her head to look up at the strain on Adam's

face, his profile carved out of granite. He must have sensed her stare; he turned to her, capturing her gaze.

There, for a brief, telling second, she witnessed the utter pain and rejection blaring in his green eyes.

It yanked her back to yesteryear when she couldn't fathom his occasional sullen moods and would watch the dark shadows shift in his eyes.

Hurt! Adam hurt then and was hurting now.

How could she have not known it then?

A niggle of guilt, along with a wave of shame, pressed behind her ribs. She'd been so young and foolish she'd missed this highly important nugget about Adam.

Without thinking, Molly reached out and grabbed Adam's wrist—warm and strong and making her skin tingle—because his fingers were curled into tight fists. She tugged him. "What took you so long? Geez, a girl could starve from waiting."

His resistance soon fell away. By slow degrees, she sensed him shucking off the tension, layer by layer.

"You invited him to our dinner?" Gemma's voice croaked.

"A guy's gotta eat, right?" Molly didn't let go of Adam until he relaxed enough to join her, sliding in the booth. His knee brushed hers. Her blood hummed in her veins. *This is crazy!*

"Some grip you got there, tiger." The rough underlining tone was for her ears only. The few words held relief and thankfulness.

Molly's chest squeezed. Her fingertips still prickled from

his hammering pulse point she'd accidentally touched and now so did her eyes with a smarting of tears. If she'd been brave enough, she'd have opened his hand and drawn a heart there, like they used to do when they shared a special bond and wanted to give comfort. "You're buying, Mr. Big Shot." If he could afford to pay her five times as much as his first quote then certainly he could cover a meal.

Adam chuckled. The raw, scratchy sound spoke volumes.

It also seemed to crack the hard stance the townspeople had taken. Now, they were released from whatever spell and back to ordering, eating, or chatting amicably.

Sean returned to his seat, a little on edge as he and Gemma shot covert looks at one another.

Picking up the slick new red-and-white menus, Molly handed them out. She popped hers open, barely seeing the words. She randomly chose something surely any Italian restaurant would offer. "I'll have, um, the spaghetti and meatballs."

"Better get the blender out," Adam teased her, grabbing her attention as she noted a hint of a smile lifting the corners of his mouth.

Her heart skipped a beat at that sexy look she remembered so well.

Gemma and Sean chuckled at the old joke.

"Those are fighting words, Larson." A little tug of glee shot through Molly. He'd remembered her penchant.

"Saves on the slicing and dicing with the fork and knife until you get the little bite size pieces."

"It tastes the same. Just less mess." She continued their

long, good-natured argument.

So, it was a childhood holdover from her overzealous parents and fear of her choking. Yeah, but twenty plus years? Okay, so sometimes she was as bad as her folks.

"No garlic bread or breath."

"Kills the romance after…" Adam stilled, tensing.

Molly blinked, recalling who watched them intently. "Words of wisdom for Gemma and Sean, right?"

"Of course."

"We're good. Really." Under the table, Gemma kicked Molly's shin.

"Ow. Geez." Molly rubbed the sore spot. "Sean, does she do that to you?"

"Worse. She headbutts me." His deadpan answer broke the last block of ice.

Joining in the round of laughter, Molly sighed inwardly.

She had no clue as to why she'd want to make Adam comfortable, but she had.

It had nothing to do with teaming up with him, for business or anything else for that matter.

Of course not. She was so over the idea, if not him just yet…

Wait. Hold up. Did I just think that?

Chapter Six

"THANKS. I OWE you." Adam held the door open two hours later as Molly exited in front of him.

The noisy atmosphere—filled with jangling silverware, shuffling plates, mouthwatering scents and food, busy staff, and jolly conversations—dimmed as they left and the barrier closed behind them, trapping the lively sounds.

In the early evening hours, the chill in the crisp air swept over him, cleansing the bad taste from earlier.

"No favors allowed, Larson." Molly checked the road and, when all was clear, marched across the street and down a door or two on the other sidewalk.

Adam jammed his hands in his jean pockets and followed. He smiled at her purposeful strides, trying to escape him. Thankfully, she hadn't shut him out back there. In front of her family and friends, she'd set the tone of his homecoming.

It could have gone so very wrong.

Because of Molly it hadn't.

Standing in front of her shop, she turned to him with her arms wrapped around her as he approached.

Clearly, this was a defensive position. Against him.

He ignored it. Instead, Adam gazed at her darkened business beyond the windows. There were eerie shadows of tripods, sectioned-off areas, backdrops, and large light shields—like umbrellas. The window displays, lit with low beams, were typical for a photography studio, smiling family and faces.

"Where's the places, Moll? Your specialty." It bothered him she hadn't pursued her love of all things beautiful and natural, buildings and landscapes. Maybe that was why she was on his mind so much with this rebuild. Everything was perfect for what she hungered for. Even right down to the wedding-themed spot.

"I don't display them…or everything I do." Her tone bristled with more defensiveness.

"Too bad. I remember the pictures you took of the old high school for our yearbook. We were the last graduating class from there and you captured the essence of that worn out, faded red brick building with all the arches and niches. I don't know, like you honored it while keeping it in a time capsule for all of us. You won a photography contest with that one." He shook his head wistfully.

"You…remembered." She swallowed hard.

"That and a lot more." This time he cleared his choked throat. "Back there." He tilted his head to the busy restaurant they'd just come from. "You didn't have to."

"No. I didn't." She drew in a long breath. "The beef I have with you is mine. My family, even the townspeople, are not involved. And they shouldn't take it out on you."

Adam braced himself. "Want to talk about said beef?" He prayed she didn't. He had no idea what he'd say or how to say anything at all. *You were special. I wasn't.*

"Let's not and say we did. How's that?"

"Works for the moment." Relief flooded through him. Adam rubbed his neck. There'd be a time when he'd have to—before he left again.

"So, this is good night." She stuck a thumb over her shoulder at her business. "Lots of things to do."

"Including an answer for me." He didn't think his heartbeat could slam any harder inside his chest. "You know, my earlier offer."

"Not ready."

A tiny smile inched up the corners of his mouth. He'd been the one to tell her that time and time again when things had gotten heated between them. *She wasn't ready.* "Sounds familiar."

"Hey, hey, hey. No memory lane stuff anymore. Why complicate a simple business transaction?"

Her words said one thing and yet he could see the longing in her eyes, even as she backed away. She bumped into the door. "Owie."

"My poor Molly." The statement rushed out before he could reel them back in.

She'd banged, dinged, and bruised herself every time she'd gotten jittery around him. It made him even more humble and protective of her than ever.

"There you go again." She turned swiftly, fumbling with jangling keys—even dropping them. Her low curse word dropped in the air.

"Tsk. Tsk." Adam grinned at her spicy language and then reached down and grabbed the offending object. "Here, I've got it."

"As if." She snagged them away quickly. Using them, she unlocked it, shoved open the moisture-swelled door, and then slammed it in his face.

"I can fix that. It won't take any time at all to plane it down."

She glared at him—the pane of glass sandwiched between them. "Not going to happen."

"The deal or the door?"

"Maybe both. Who knows?"

"I'll just wait here for you to let me know."

Molly stomped away, leaving him grinning from ear-to-ear.

Of course, he'd stay to annoy the heck out of her. Now that the parking rules changed after five for Vine Street, he'd get his pickup truck and move it in front of her shop.

It might prove to be a long night, but well worth the effort in the end.

At least Adam hoped it would turn out in his favor…

YES, THANK YOU, *he's gone.* Molly breathed a sigh of relief when she peeked out from behind the counter.

Adam, along with his shadow, were nowhere to be found outside her shop. Arcs of lights from the street lanterns revealed mostly a trickle of traffic by vehicles and more by foot.

None were his tall, lean familiar frame.

A pinch of regret pinged her conscience.

In spite of how the evening had started, Adam had been witty and charming, regaling Gemma, Sean, and her with his many escapades on his building projects—the buried or sealed-off objects he'd found, how many near disasters he or his crew had avoided, and plenty of wild episodes of rushing to completion in the nick of time.

Interspersed, they reminisced about school, beloved and hated teachers, hair-raising football games, dances, and numerous memorable moments captured.

There was so many good, heartwarming times.

And only one really, really bad time. She blanked that one out tonight, longing to be normal for the first time in ages.

Just two couples enjoying delicious food and great conversation, right?

She could almost forget. She could almost imagine this night was one of many they'd gone on with her brother and his future wife.

Yeah, that bride thing brought it all back.

If only Molly could move on. Okay, maybe Adam had done them both a favor—

"Who am I kidding here?"

The sound of a truck slowing down captured her complete, undivided attention. Its brakes squealed to a halt right in front of her shop, blocking her view.

"What the hey?"

She scrambled from where she sat perched on the edge of her stool—because she hadn't been able to gather her senses enough to settle into work.

Hitting the floor, she strode to the front of her studio, gazing out in wonder. "Adam Larson, what do you think you're doing? You can't park there!"

He jumped out of the cab, slamming the door shut, and then rounded the bed. With dexterity, Adam hopped into the back of the truck. All the while, he grinned in her direction.

"Wh-what are you doing?" She charged out the instant she realized he was bedding down, moving things and lying there. Molly strode to the truck, clamped her hands around the edge, and peered over and down at him.

Adam lay back on a huge black duffel bag with his hands clasped behind his head and one foot crossed over the other, smiling up at her. "Come to kiss me good-night?"

"As if! You can't sleep here."

"Watch me."

"It's not legal."

"Sign says no parking between nine a.m. and five p.m. It's after." He wiggled, getting comfy. "Ah, pretty night, too."

He was nonchalant and obstinate—more than ever before—and sexy as all heck. His broad shoulders stretched his white button-down shirt, straining the button part. Even from here, she felt the warmth and heat rising from his long body.

Molly gulped hard. She recalled his strong arms holding her, and the way he'd chase the chill from deep inside her bones. And he'd banished her doubts, every last one of them, through the years.

Her protector. Her love.

"You're...blocking my business."

"None to speak of at this hour."

Exasperation filled her chest and spurted out. "Do you have an answer for everything?"

"Seems so. Try me again."

"I'm calling the police."

"Never been arrested before. Close, though. If I'm being hauled in tonight so are you."

"Me?" Her voice squeaked. "I haven't done anything wrong."

"Says who?" He shifted, so his gaze captured hers, pinning her to the spot. "It should be illegal to look like an angel. Now that your hair is down, the light from the moon is all around your head, making it look like a halo. And your eyes. God, I dream about getting so lost in the bluest of blue. Gossamer. Ethereal. Someone not of this world, Moll."

His soft, whispered words caressed her. Molly swayed slightly, thrust back years when he'd talk to her like this. Sweet. Meaningful. Heart-achingly beautiful.

If she wasn't careful, he'd pull her back and under again...

Chapter Seven

"YOU'RE IMPOSSIBLE, ADAM." She choked out the words from her clogged, parched throat. Why was he doing this after years of dead silence?

She recalled the driven, determined part of him that would stop at nothing in school—to prove himself. Had he transferred it to his business dealings? Most likely by the obvious success he'd earned. Was that what this was all about? Getting her to sign a contract?

On trembling legs, she shoved away, pivoted, and then walked back into her shop. With a firm click, she locked the door behind her.

So what if he's out there all night. So what if he gets cold.

Molly tried to harden her heart. But pin prickles poked at her chest as if the organ buried deep inside was coming out of a long sleep.

"No! Don't be ridiculous. Pretty words from the mouth of a liar? And suddenly I'm caving here? Not on your life. Correction. Not on *my* life."

With burning determination swirling inside her, Molly set to work on autopilot. There were fifty or more pictures of the triplets to scour through on the memory cards—hoping to find a gem among the less cooperative ones and a treasure in the dress-up, playful ones.

Then there were the others—Adam's new venture. *Wedding venue.*

Molly's cheeks grew warm. Longing wound through her. She hadn't been so excited and snapping with ideas in ages—since before he'd left her.

She sucked in a painful breath.

"My life. Divided. Before that day Adam left. And since then. Two distinct halves to a damaged whole."

The troubling thoughts tugged at her throughout the careful process of her time-consuming work. Hours flew by and a part of her delighted in the details—thrilled to discover she'd not only had gotten the best shot for Kyle and Kyra, several for the triplets, a dozen for the Pickens's property, and one heart-stopping, breath-stealing one of Adam leaning against the barn frame and looking at the lens—staring into her soul.

Molly gasped, jerking up and away from the image as if putting distance between her and it would erase what she swore she read there. "No. Not true."

She shook her head, stood abruptly, and came around the corner. His white company truck was still there in the early morning hours. The streetlight arched over the back half of the bed, allowing her to see the misty rain coming down.

Her belly twisted. It had to be in the forties. Cold and wet. "He's out there in this?"

Without another thought, she hustled to close down her programs, box light, and safely store everything away, tidying up. Molly grabbed her camera, stuffed it in the protective case, and then slung it around her neck. In less than ten minutes, she walked out the door.

Her footsteps dragged the closer she got to the truck bed. She found him awake and shivering, partly under a blue tarp, arms crossed over his chest. *You don't give up, do you, Adam? So why did you when it came to us?*

It was on the tip of her tongue to drag him into the shop and get him warm.

"Fancy meeting you here." Adam grinned.

Her heart squeezed. "Just so you know, I'm going home now."

Adam shucked off the tarp, wiped the back of his hand over his face, and jumped up. "I'll give you a ride."

"No need. Mine's at the town parking square around the corner."

"Get in." He went to the side of the bed and with his hand on the rail, jumped down. Adam stood less than a foot away.

Her insides quivered at the closeness. However, her guilty conscience nagged at her to get him out of this chilly, wet weather. "I can walk." She did a one eighty and stalked off.

There were familiar noises behind her—his footsteps, the cab door opening and slamming shut, the engine starting, and then the brakes squealing alongside of her.

Wait! That last one. She jerked to stare at him as he

crawled the truck along beside her. The passenger-side window was down.

"Going my way, angel?"

Something soft and sweet tugged in her belly. "I'm good."

"Of course you're good. But don't you want a lift?"

"Nope." She put one foot in front of the other, her boots hitting the sidewalk in a steady rhythm eating up the cobble-stoned way.

That didn't deter Adam. No, he followed along, still talking. "Can't change your mind?"

The mist picked up to a slow drizzle, covering her in a slick sheen. She remained silently stoic, marching now to the end of Vine Street and then taking the right onto Main.

Not missing a beat, Adam turned the truck, matching her steps.

The moment she spotted her SUV snuggly in her familiar spot, she picked up her pace. Nothing shook him from her trail; he even motored into the parking square and waited for her to get in and start it up.

A ribbon of wonder stroked through Molly at how much she'd missed someone caring enough about her—no, Adam, caring so darn much about her—to protect her and keep her safe.

"You're recovering, remember?" she gently scolded herself.

With the soft purr of her engine beneath her and the vents on warm to clear the frost covering her windows, Molly sat for a moment, highly aware of the idling truck nearby.

Adam.

How could you be so you *right now? How could one simple act stir me to my toes again?*

Her breath shivered out of her. Molly brushed back her damp hair, attempting to collect herself. Once she eased her SUV out of the spot, curved the steering wheel to go around the area, turned right onto Main, she'd stopped shaking.

Maybe it was Adam's presence behind her, following her all the way home.

In less than fifteen minutes, she pulled into her parents' long driveway, until she halted in front of the garage—and her upstairs apartment.

The usual spotlight at the pitch of the twenty-foot roof only shone one way. "One bulb out. Must call Sean about it. He's got the long ladder and won't hear of his baby—emphasis on the baby part—sister tackling it. Mom and Dad would have a fit if their preemie even tried."

The shadows grew when she shut her lights off.

It made the loneliness crawl in a little deeper.

No one waited for her there. No light in her window beaconed her home.

Funny how Adam stayed true to form, waiting for her, like he used to when they were dating. She did everything in reverse, shoving her vehicle into park, and then the engine.

She climbed out, closing the door behind her. Standing there, she knew this was as far as he was going.

A niggling thought scratched her mind. She slung her camera bag into place and strode to his truck door. Her mouth went dry as his window came down. To be so close to him now.

"Thanks." Her teeth chattered. "You have a place, don't you?"

"The carriage house at Pickens's farm."

Her heart twisted as the image of that decrepit building from earlier in the day. "Is that even livable?" Did it have heat and running water?

"Barely. But it's not the worst place I've ever bunked down in." There was a roughness in his voice.

"Look." She grit her teeth. "I can stay at my folks'." She tilted her head to the empty house. They wouldn't be back for weeks. "You can…you know, have mine until you find something better."

She kicked herself to all ways to Sunday in her head for that offer.

Adam jerked his head back and then shook it. "Couldn't possibly…" He cleared his throat. "The gossip and rumors."

Molly felt the weight of his words. He was protecting her. Again.

"'Night, Molly." He turned his head, his profile to her. "You're just getting wetter and wetter the longer you wait."

"So this is one way, right? As usual. You get to do this for me, but I don't for you. I'm not a lovesick teenager any-more." That slipped out. *The* L *word, really, in front of him? Another half dozen minus points in the invisible hopeless romantic recovery log of mine.*

"Good." His word came out curt and clipped. "Don't act like one then." His challenge sat between them, hot and heavy. "Grow up and take the damn job. Your business needs it. *You* need it."

"Don't look a gift horse in the mouth, is that it?" How could she have felt sorry for him one minute and ticked off by him the very next?

The muscle in Adam's jaw jerked. He turned to her, his green eyes cold and hard. "It's not a gift. It's called work. You want more? Earn it. You pull this off—documenting the progression, input for the renovations, taking the contract as the lead photographer—and I'll hand over twenty-five percent."

"The profits?" *Whoa, that's big money.* But how did he know so much about her lackluster outcome so far and her circumstances? She'd snatched up the tempting lease on the property in the heart of Cupid's Corner and poured everything into it, trying to prove a point to herself and her family. *Yeah, how's that working for you?*

"Of the entire business, Moll."

She swallowed hard. The breath in her lungs stayed trapped there, fighting to break free through the burning. He dangled a dream of hers right in front of her very eyes. Long ago, she'd wanted this very thing—bringing happiness to couples on their big days. "You…can't be serious."

"Never more so."

"I don't know what to say, Adam, or why you're doing this." He offered her hope. She didn't know what to do with it; it had been missing for so long from her life.

"Yes would be the correct answer." The slight tug at the corners of his mouth nearly brought her to her knees. "Ten a.m. See you then."

"Make it eleven in three days and I'll let you know then." She had a jam-packed schedule this week and needed more time to process it all.

"Do you really have to think about it?" He nodded. "Yeah, I guess when I'm the other seventy-five-percent owner, you do."

The sliver of sadness crept into his tone and weaved through her.

Adam powered up his window, clearly and effectively calling it a night.

With what seemed like lead in her steps, Molly walked to the side wooden outside steps. She stopped at the bottom to turn. He was there, lights on, and waiting.

Her mind pounded with thoughts and questions as she climbed the twenty-two stairs, hanging on to the slick, wooden railing as she went. She tugged open the squeaky screen door, found her keys with cold, shaky hands, and then unlocked the door.

Darkness greeted her as she let the door bang closed behind her. She gently placed her camera bag on the nearby foyer bench, shucked off soggy boots, and then ran a hand over her wet face and through soaked hair.

Still Adam didn't move; the headlights remained focused and steady.

Molly rushed to the large front window overlooking the driveway. She reached out and tugged on the pull lamp string. Soft, yellowy light spilled nearby. Outside, Adam flicked his headlights off, on, off, and then on again before he eased out in reverse.

Their code.

She sucked in a long, slow, shivery breath.

He'd unnerved her. Then. Now. Always.

And her poor, aching heart squeezed again as she watched him back onto the street and then pull away.

You were supposed to be this monster I made up in my head after you left me. Not this guy. Not the funny, sweet, caring Adam I knew and loved once…

Chapter Eight

ADAM STOOD IN the center of chaos—trucks beeping as they backed up, his foreman in full-on mode, half his two dozen crew members directing drivers to drop the loads of reclaimed lumber in the designated spot, the rest in the barn clearing debris, and guys shouting back and forth.

He stood at the back of his truck, tailgate down, and blueprints spread out after seeing off the city permit guy.

Old man Pickens dragged a hand through his scraggly gray beard as he drew near. "Haven't seen it hopping like this since we harvested the last crop pert near three years ago."

"It'll look worse before it gets better, friend." Something nudged Adam. Was it too much for the guy? He did seem dazed since they'd gotten straight to work the day after Adam arrived. Watching his home—at least the property—torn up and ripped apart had to be gut-wrenching. "I got a couple errands in town for you, if you're up to it."

"Sure thing. Can't be of much use around here now, can I?"

"I'd say you've helped plenty already." Adam tilted his head to the departing white car—its tires crunching the gravel under them. "I was happy to see you knew him and smoothed a few wrinkles for me." He'd shaved a few days off the paperwork and approvals. "Worth your weight in gold already." He grinned.

Pickens chuckled. "I got the gift of gab, my mom said. Works most times."

Adam scratched down a list of items from the local hardware store to tide them over before the larger supplies showed up and handed it over. "I need these to make the upper floor of the carriage house livable while I'm staying there."

He'd hunkered down in a sleeping bag on the hard floor the last three nights. But he did draw the line at not having usable facilities—hiking to the main house each morning. He tugged out his wallet and pulled out five one-hundred-dollar bills and then handed them over.

Pickens whistled low and long. "Ben sure is looking good these days." He rolled it up nice and neat, along with the list, and eased them in the top pocket of his denim jacket, securing the snap.

"Comes in handy, doesn't he?" There were times, not too many years ago, when Adam went weeks, even months, without seeing the face on that denomination.

"I'll say." Pickens tapped the back of the truck, metal pinging. "I best be getting going." As he turned to leave, he halted at the sound of gravel crunching again.

Adam jerked around, breath stuck in his throat. In the back of his mind, he'd been waiting for this moment. She didn't disappoint.

"That pretty little Molly's here." The older man cocked his head and then his eyebrow. "She need me to stay?"

Funny how he asked it like that. "Not that I know of, but you can always ask her yourself."

There was nothing he'd do to hurt her again. But try telling that to the good people in Cupid's Corner.

"Got my answer. I'll be off now." He strolled away toward the approaching SUV and then met up with it. "Fine day, Miss Molly."

From here, Adam couldn't hear anything, but he did see her wave to Pickens.

With his heart hammering away in his chest, Adam waited for her. *Thug. Thug.* He watched her park off to the side near the scraggly lawn, exit her vehicle, and then walk his way.

She was his Molly and yet she wasn't. A grown-up version of the shy, innocent girl he'd fallen head over heels for.

Adam gulped, watching her with her shoulders back, spine straight, determination in every long-legged stride. Her red hair, now below her shoulders, danced in the slight breeze and the sunglasses she wore covered her beautiful blue eyes—however, he remembered every detail of them in his dreams and even now. In skinny jeans and dusty boots and with a curve-skimming pale-blue shirt on, she could give runway models a run for their money.

But Molly would rather be behind the camera than in front of it. Any day of the week.

She didn't like the spotlight or attention on herself. That was why this was a dicey proposition to hand to her.

Now, would she take it…

When she got within two feet of him, she whipped off her glasses and plunked them on top of her head. Her unwavering stare nailed him.

This was new and welcome. His heart rate went into overdrive.

Molly stuck out her hand.

He took it, liking the strength in her slender grip. Heat sparked and traveled up his arm. He bit down hard on a groan.

"Deal is, I'll document this reno." She lifted her chin a notch higher. "I'll even take the wedding shots. This summer to start and only if the couples agree. I don't want your pity percentage, Adam."

She could have knocked him over with a feather. "Pity?" God, she was incredibly smart and saw right through him. "It's more of a payday. One I couldn't provide for you then, but can now."

When she tried to pull away, Adam held tight, longing to keep the connection to her and that wave of warmth rippling through his cold body.

"I didn't want your money." Her jaw clamped down, tension rolling off her and to him in that touch.

He watched the streak of anger flash through her eyes—white hot—and then disappear, snuffed out, until hurt followed with a dewy look.

"I didn't have any to give you at the time, so good thing I decided for both of us then." How could she not see it? Not thank him for not dragging her down to his level back then? Struggling for every dime for years and years growing up wore a person down. She never experienced that.

Finally, she yanked her hand away, shaking it as if to get the feeling back, and then grabbing on to her ever present camera on the strap around her neck. "Yeah, good thing. God only knows where we'd be now."

The sarcasm of hers sliced his chest, ripping it open. "Glad we got that out of the way. And don't think I'm going to let that percentage thing go." He owed her. Why wouldn't she take what he was giving?

"Dream on, Larson. I can't be bought." She swallowed hard. "I work for a living."

A heap of admiration streamed through Adam. He liked the slightly tougher Molly, more stubborn and direct, who stood up for what she thought was right.

It went against what he'd wanted, but there was plenty of time to show her his way was the right way. "And our fake reunion. It goes with the deal. Free publicity. For both of our businesses."

She grunted.

"I take that as a yes."

"You will not best me, Larson, understand? That's a no. *N-o.*"

Whoa now! She was sugar when he'd known her, but now the spice was showing. Full on.

He might have a more difficult time then he first thought...

Chapter Nine

FIVE HOURS LATER, Molly's finger hurt, her hands cramped, and her eyes grew sore and gritty. But she'd never been more excited at the images she'd captured—shapes, lines, angles, the sun-bleached metal rooster weather vane haphazardly crooked and reset temporarily on top of the pitched roof—a sign of renewal, sun peeking through the barn doors and glinting off the antique tractor parts sticking out of tufts of leftover hay…

She'd gone from challenging Adam to being challenged in a space of ten minutes of arriving and hadn't let up since.

From the moment she'd seen him again days ago until she'd confronted him, she could not, would not stop thinking of him. Long hours of tossing and turning and dedicated hard work allowed her to consider his offer.

No matter how many times she'd tried to refute it, she always came back to the same shocking conclusion.

This was his way to say sorry. Although he'd said the words, his actions spoke in thunderous volume.

Why would someone as successful as Adam now return to his hometown to risk this crazy, expensive adventure?

Cupid's Corner—off the beaten path—did have the love vibe going on; however, it wasn't on anyone's radar other than for Valentine's Day festivities.

He was creating a wedding niche where there was none.

A very costly, intensive undertaking that might or might not take off or pay off in the end.

Molly had searched the internet for every scrap of knowledge about Adam—which was little—and his company—which was a great deal. Nowhere did he actually permanently acquire one of his renovated buildings. No, he bought, fixed, and then flipped them. Or he was hired on by prestigious organizations to remodel their places. Not once had Adam kept a business, other than his own construction company. Until now.

The pieces she'd inspected had fallen into place.

Adam had done the impossible by buying the Pickens place instead of it falling into the developer's hands—plowing down the old buildings and carving up the precious land. And then Adam pushed to have it turned into an events center, leaving it mostly intact as he set about improving it.

He'd taken everything she'd loved and put them all together, presenting her a perfect package. And the darn pity percentage.

Deep inside her, he astonished her with his gift. And scared her to death.

Because Adam knew her, better than anyone had ever gotten to know her, including her best friend and her own family. Taking this would be an admission, many tiny and big, clumped together.

Apology accepted? Hurts bandaged? Wounds healed?

If that were so, where would that leave them?

She knew. The thrown in ridiculous offer of a fake reunion would end—in reverse—with her saying no to him. He'd be free to go. Forever this time.

Her, though? She'd come to live in the knowledge, accept it, take it for granted that she was hurt irrevocably and he'd been the cause—the bruised identity she'd held on to for nearly six years gone for good.

Letting go of it once and for all.

Now he wanted to make amends—real, solid, and impressive. How could she hold anything against him ever again? Who and what would she be without Adam and his indelible imprint in her scarred heart and battered soul?

CLIMBING TREES OR truck hoods to get a better shot hadn't been in Molly's normal realm of photography, yet she took to it like bees to honey.

Exhilaration hummed in her veins even now as she stood near the edge of the pond at her back and aimed the lens at this side of the old weathered barn. Its height and breadth stole her breath away.

In her mind's eye, she pictured the changes—trees trimmed back, brush gone, barn warming in the afternoon sun. Inside, the thick beams exposed, cleared out or cleaned up, glittering chandeliers with dangling crystals, polished wood floors, tables set with crisp, white china and shiny silverware and sparkling wineglasses, sweet-smelling multi-colored flowers drooping from centerpieces, and lit candles glowing on each table gathering the intimacy of the special moment even closer.

Her breath hitched at the image.

No, you can't do that. No salivating over the weddings. You're not going down that path. Not. At. All.

"Hello, you're in recovery, remember?" Molly yanked her lens away and focused on another line—shorter, squatter, yet distinctive in its own right—of the carriage house. From this angle, she admired the sturdiness of the old gal.

Peeking out of the second-story opening, Adam came into sight.

This time her heart thwacked in her chest. Her mouth went dry.

"Geez, you'd think I'd learn by now."

"Come on up!" He took off his white hardhat and waved to her with it. "You'll love the view from here."

Those are fighting words.

He knew exactly what tapped into her longings. *Not fair.*

She trudged up the incline of the hill, berating the tug of longing and prickly sensations skittering through her body as he watched her. Too intently for her liking.

A good ten minutes later, Molly lifted one foot after the other up the creaking carriage house wooden stairs.

Adam was there, at the top, waiting for her. Broad, lean, and with the intense look and a slight smile he wore it all so well.

How could he be even more handsome? She snatched up her camera and took a shot. Some things were better on film than committed to memory. Adam, for one. Well, that was if she discounted the gorgeous flesh and blood man himself.

"I'd have thought you'd have enough of me by now."

She shrugged as she gained the last step and tilted her head back to gaze at him. A shiver of awareness skimmed along her veins.

He'd been a dream to photograph. She'd taken dozens and dozens of him through high school. First on the pretense of needing football players' photos, to simple ones of students hanging out, to images for the yearbook, and then to when he finally asked her out in tenth grade and began dating her.

"You're staring."

"So are you." He barely moved his lips.

Her eyes landed there, wondering if he tasted even better than before. *Yeah, like that's possible.*

"Why, Adam? Why did you leave?" *Me. Why did you leave* me?

"We're doing this now?"

"As good a time as any." But it wasn't.

She steeled herself. This wouldn't be easy to hear. However, it was necessary for her to process it all before moving forward, or more than she had already, on this project.

"I told you then."

"You didn't want to hold me back." How funny! If only she could laugh about it. She was far worse now than she was then.

Adam stared at her intently for a half dozen heartbeats.

Something strained between them, stretching and yearning.

He turned and walked to the open carriage doors.

She glimpsed the large, stark rustic space around her. One lone wooden chair—with peeling white paint—stood in the corner with a rolled-up red-and-black-checked sleeping bag propped up beside it, his large black duffel bag close by, and a short stack of books took up prime residence on the seat. A wave of sharp empathy at his barren existence swept over her, making her ache down to her bones.

"I promised you a view, didn't I?" His voice came out low and rough.

She stared at his ramrod straight back and stiff shoulders. He could have been carved in stone for all the stillness in him. Sometimes, like now, she wondered if he had granite in his veins instead of blood.

Gosh, Adam. What happened? To you? To what we had?

Molly took slow, measured steps toward Adam, wondering how tension could vibrate in the air like it took on a life of its own. When she halted beside him, she gazed at the most incredible sight.

From here, she could see for miles—down the slope of the hill, to the pond, over the calm water, to the park, the adorable heart bridge, and over the buildings of Cupid's Corner. "This...is stunning." She lifted her hand and clutched the frame, allowing the quiet beauty to seep into every fiber of her.

By slow degrees, Adam relaxed. "No pictures?"

"I…" How could she explain this feeling? "Want to soak it all in." *In real time. Not from behind a barrier or shield.* Her gaze swept over all the familiar places, yet saw them for the first time. Each layer sunk in—the strokes and lines and angles—as if it were a painting she'd seen once before but not at all. "It's the same, yet different."

"Like us, Moll."

There it was. Somehow he made her see it. "I was so—"

"Young."

"*Naive* is a better description." *Dramatic, too.* She dragged in a breath and then another, her fingers curling into the sun-warmed wood.

"I wasn't good for you."

"That's not true, Adam." She squeezed her eyes shut for a brief moment. "You were real and right and…made me feel beautiful."

He chuckled. "You were. Still are."

Molly turned and leaned a shoulder on the frame, feeling the warm breeze skim along her skin. It felt like Adam had reached out and caressed her cheek.

Adam took a similar stance on the other side, allowing his gaze to meet and hold hers. "Don't doubt us and what we had then."

"I have since you left. How could we be so far apart when we'd been so close?"

"As much as it—" Adam halted, blowing out a breath. He dragged a hand through his hair. "It hurt, make no mistake about it. But it had to be done."

"For me? Making decisions without me again?" Something rumbled inside her. Everyone did that for her, thinking she was too weak or didn't know her own mind or what was in own her best interest. She hated it.

"Us. Molly, I was going to sap every beautiful thing from you. A wife? I couldn't even take care of myself. I couldn't afford college then."

"You're not making sense." Money had been tight, even a struggle for his family and him, but he'd overcome the tuition part. "You won that football scholarship. You and I would have worked for the extra fees not covered."

"I blew the scholarship by point five."

A streak of dawning rippled through her, tearing her apart. He'd hidden that from her. "You never told me."

"Why disappoint you more?" He jerked his gaze to the view, although, she doubted he saw much by the way he curled his hands into fists.

Pressure slammed into her chest. "That's pretty lame, don't you think?" The least he could have done was tell her the truth then.

"For missing out by that slim of a chance? Yep."

"Not that." Molly hugged her arms around her, clamping the camera to her. *Yeah, another imprint—death by camera. More like bleeding heartache.* So many things were shards of them, cracked and broken, like glass. "You didn't trust *us* to survive."

The words tumbled out and shocked her own ears. *The ring of truth.*

"Money matters."

"Wait! You sound like—"

"Mr. McCleary, the accountant. He did us a favor by showing me the numbers. Do you know how little I could give you then? Even if you went on to college and we found a place off campus. No construction work in the winter. Long hours and hard work the rest of the time. Pennies, on a good month."

"My…dad talked to you. When?" Shock thudded in her chest.

"All along. I wouldn't listen. Not until I got the letter saying I lost the scholarship. I think they call that a rude awakening."

"Yeah, tell me about it."

Adam jerked his gaze to her and then he fully turned, nabbing her elbow so she faced him, too. The warmth of his fingers sparked along her skin. He let go, but not before he trailed his fingertips down her arm, stopping short of taking her hand.

Molly shivered. At the touch and the warring emotions battling in his darkening green eyes. Deep down, behind the confusion, she noted the flash of pain that came and went.

He's hiding again. Something we both do. The thought fired and spread. *In different ways, but we both keep things under wrap.*

"I couldn't do that to you, Molly. And I couldn't watch your starry-eyed hero worship slowly fade and then die over time. Every day a little bit more of that crushed look would seep into your soul—your sweet, gentle soul." His voice cracked. "I didn't want to disappoint you…"

Suddenly, she recalled visiting his parents' house once

LAURIE LeCLAIR

after many invitations to Sunday dinner. Of course, she'd met the reserved couple at football games and occasionally in Cupid's Corner, but never spent time at their simple, humble home.

Adam had been antsy and agitated for days leading up to it, even trying to get her to not go.

Then she'd been shy, quiet, and observant. Something bothered him about her being there. It wasn't until the end of the pleasant enough, delicious home-cooked meal that she'd figured it out. Bits and pieces of jumbled conversation clicked into place like a kaleidoscope, allowing her to understand.

His mother had been the bright one, forgoing a higher education to appease his father's vanity, or lack of intellectual skills—although, he'd been a darn good carpenter. The best in the county, most proclaimed. Mrs. Larson lived a life of need. At one point, she never even realized she'd done it; she gazed at her husband as he held court and sighed deeply.

"Sh-she didn't waste her life, Adam." The words stuck in her throat.

He was trying to save me from that life of exiled desperation…

Chapter Ten

A DAM STAYED BUSY the next days as the team—camped out during the work week for the duration in company-owned travel trailers on another plot of Pickens's land Adam had bought and always at the ready—jacked up the barn to level it again, poured the new foundation, and waited for it to set properly. In the meantime, he'd instructed the cleanup and the first round of landscaping—brush cutting, dead tree removal, and a path cleared for a construction road onto and in the property to maneuver the many trucks coming back and forth.

At nights, he'd divided his time between adjusting the plans as they dug deeper into the renovations, made new discoveries that needed repair, had his executive assistant, Mrs. Sanderson, line up the local plumbing and electrician contractors, redid the second floor of the carriage house into a livable space, and study.

Construction company owner by day. Third year college student by night.

Through all of it, he tried to shake Molly's sane and sensible argument. Maybe he hadn't given her enough credit to endure the hardships that were sure to follow. But he couldn't chance losing her respect when he couldn't protect her from the harsh reality of failure.

More like seeing the love fade and die away in her eyes…

Either way, right or wrong, he had to live with his decision. Now, he could do something tangible for her, help her get on her feet and make a success out of her photography studio.

She deserved so much more and he was doing everything in his power to give her a dream to hold on to when he left again…

Now, in the early morning hours, as he walked into the heart of sleepy Cupid's Corner from where he'd parked his truck in the town lot, he blinked as if he'd been transported back in time.

"Same, but different. No, I'm the one who's changed."

His heart tugged. Memories rushed back. Even though half the businesses along Main were being remodeled, the layers of metal scaffolding didn't take away from the old familiar haunts.

There'd been plenty of times he'd stop by Valentine's At Vine after football practice or on the way home from an after-school construction gig to see Molly at her part-time job. The Valentine family, especially Grams, would welcome him with open arms, offering him plates of her delicious homemade cookies. He was partial to her infamous big, heart-shaped sugar cookies. Gramps regaled him with the history of the building or one of the antiques presently for sale.

It was one of the few times he felt as if he truly belonged. The sweet, older couple were one of his favorites in town. He'd have to make a point of going to see them, maybe even get some pointers on where to find a few decent pieces for the carriage house and barn. He'd hold off on the old Victorian house until the winter—long after he left town—to refurbish it and get the Valentines' help.

Back then, Gemma would make faces at Sean, who hefted and hauled boxes and furniture for the antiques shop. They'd fuss and argue, too.

Adam chuckled. "Who would have thought those two would ever get along, never mind be getting married?"

Something dropped in his gut. Envy? Disgust at himself for leaving his girl, Molly, behind? "Maybe both."

He shook his head out of the past and trudged down the cobblestone sidewalk, intentionally avoiding cutting back and going down Vine to pop in on Molly at her studio.

"That's why I'm here, remember?"

Another ten, then I will.

Up ahead, he spotted the Sugar Shack. Years ago, he'd grab some candy and save it for class breaks, sharing with Molly. He'd gotten her to try his favorite and she'd made it a point to never let him forget it, either, because she'd fallen for it, too.

"Perfect peace offering." He headed to the store a few doors down.

Because, Larson, you need to give her something. The other day, she'd surprised him with her direct request on why he'd left. Torn between sugarcoating things or the truth, he landed hard on the wrong side of right.

Adam blew out a pent-up breath.

Who knew trying to make peace with what he'd done had him revisiting his decisions—good and bad?

If only I'd tried harder. Instead of giving up...

He clamped his hand on the door handle, curling his fingers around the cool metal, and then jerked it open. The bell jangled loudly, startling the occupants.

"Sorry." He nodded to the shopkeeper and to the lone customer as he quickly entered, allowing the door to ease closed behind him. "Sean?" He frowned. The rows and rows of lined-up bins overflowing with treats assailed his senses—chocolate, cherry, even some orange. "Sweet tooth, buddy?"

Sean grinned sheepishly. "It's a thing with Gemma." He shrugged. "You?"

"You know me. Red licorice twists." He headed down that aisle, passing some tempting lemon drops and fruity slices. Adam spotted them and grabbed a small white bag nearby, snapping it open. With tongs, he dipped into the plastic cube and grabbed at least a dozen. He hesitated and then went back for more.

When he checked out, Adam realized Sean waited for him. Just what he didn't need was Molly's big brother looking at him like that—stern and questioning. They'd played football together in high school and had a decent friendship. Now, yeah, Adam didn't think so.

"Well, I can't believe my luck." The shopkeeper, Mr. Coleman, eyed them both. "Not one, but two of the players from the championship team, here in my shop. Wait right there." He scrambled to the back. Sounds of rifling through things came next. "Just a minute. I know it's here somewhere…"

Adam glanced at Sean and lifted a shoulder. "Beats me."

"Gemma told me not to say anything."

Gut punch. "But you feel the need to." *Here it comes. I should have expected this.*

"Obviously. Molly's my sister."

"She's lucky to have you and Gemma on her side." He meant it. If nothing else, he knew she'd have them to see her through the worse. Her folks and the Valentine family, too.

Sean scowled. "You weren't supposed to care anymore."

Found out. Adam shot him a half smile. "I want the best for her." *Always have. Always will.* He let a beat or three of silence go by, well, other than Mr. Coleman making rustling noises in the back. "I wasn't. The best, that is."

"So, you just thought you'd step aside and someone else would come along and take that place? No, don't answer. If there's anything I learned from writing the Dear Cupid column with Gemma is people have some messed-up ideas about relationships and love. Me, included."

Yep, guilty of that, too.

They shared an awkward laugh.

"Got it!" Mr. Coleman rushed back, waving the eight-by-ten photo. He slapped it down on the counter and then patted the edge. "Championship game. As I live and breathe, I've got the two stars right here in front of me at the same time. Can you sign it for me?"

Adam did a double take. It had been years since he'd

seen the once glossy game-day shot with Sean and him in their torn, grass-stained uniforms in front, both holding the football he'd just scored the winning touchdown with and surrounded by their teammates and coaches. A little charge went through Adam at the pride in him and on Molly's face as she'd taken the picture for the school, capturing the exhilarating moment for all time.

The day unfolded in his memory bank along with the rush of excitement and anticipation. The thrill of victory, still sharp and poignant, lingered. And that night, Adam thought for once with his hard work and dedication he could accomplish anything, so he'd asked Molly to marry him.

He swallowed down the sweet, aching moment when she'd looked at him with stars in her eyes and said yes. *Hope. Love.*

"Sure. Why not?" He took the offered marker and scribbled his name on the bottom and then handed it over to Sean, who then did the same.

"Oh, boy. I can't thank you enough for this." The older man picked up the image and grinned from ear to ear. "This is going in my trophy case. Cupid's Corner one and only championship. You boys were something else. Your arm, Sean, and your legs, Adam. No one could beat that combo. Yep, that was a special year."

In more ways than one. "Magic, sir, pure magic." Adam didn't mean football, either.

Regret washed through him.

Molly, what did I do?

You didn't trust us, she'd said.

Young love wasn't supposed to last, right?

His chest squeezed. Had it gotten everything wrong? What if he'd made the opposite choice? Where would they be now?

ADAM PARTED WAYS with Sean, inviting him out to the property to have a look around as both friend and architect.

Now, strolling to a stop in front of Molly's shop, he spotted her through the window. She was joined at the white table by a young excited couple, looking through a small stack of photos.

He stood, watching Molly's unguarded features, so caught up in the couple. There, that flash was definitely his Molly from yesteryear.

"She loves this stuff. Romance and weddings." He must have moved and caught her swift, startled attention.

For a moment, she captured his gaze. In hers, the joy slid to wonder and then a mask slipped into place. She shot him a scowl.

Adam sucked in a sharp, painful breath, knowing she'd disguised her true feelings. But he'd witnessed the glow, the unmistakable longing, and then the crash.

He dodged the last and focused on his snapping nerves, firing on all cylinders.

The past hadn't died. Nor had his feelings.

"Nah... Amends. Wanting her forgiveness. That's all this is about."

It had to be or else that would mean…

MOLLY'S BREATH STAYED trapped in her lungs as Adam, after bursting in, pulled a chair out, turned it around, and joined them.

He'd introduced himself and Kyle and Kyra were soon enamored of his presence.

Yeah, so am I.

"It's true then." Kyra giggled and glanced at Kyle. "I told you, Ky. That wasn't just gossip. Molly's sweetheart came back. Isn't that so romantic?"

Kyle's cheeks turned a little red, surely the same shade as Molly's were now.

Gossip? What could possibly go wrong with this, Larson? Molly tried to put the brakes on it. "Don't believe everything—"

"Believe it, well, that we're back together. That's true. How can we ignore the sparks? Molly's always been shy, isn't that right, honey?" Adam leaned toward her with a goofy grin on his face. "We can't keep it a secret forever, not in a small town like Cupid's Corner of all places. You know how they melt at all the love stories."

"You two?" Kyle jerked his head back and blinked. "Wow! I thought my mom and her friends were joking when they said you and Molly will have the first wedding at the renovated barn. That's so cool!"

Molly swallowed hard. Just over a week and already the

over-the-top rumors spread wild.

Adam whispered under his breath, but she heard it. "Perfect."

More like free publicity. The townspeople would go crazy with the so-called news. That web slipped another notch tighter.

"Do you mind?" Molly tried to smile, but her mouth felt stiff and awkward as her heart thumped wildly.

"Not at all." Adam snatched up the large photos and offered his unsolicited advice. "Great shots, Moll. Are you sure you two aren't models? You'd look great in our marketing brochure and on the website. Ah, these cutesy with all the hearts in town."

"Did you just say cutesy?" Molly giggled at his word choice, so unlike her strong, macho Adam. *Wait, did I just say* my *Adam?*

"Sugar sweet." He held up a hand. "Forgot." He tugged out the white paper bag stuffed in his top pocket. The familiar red licorice twist sticks poked out of the top. He held them out for her, grinning, and then waved them in front of her. "Go ahead. I know you want to."

With a shaky hand, she reached for one. "So bad of you, Larson." But her mouth watered at the treat and her heart burst at the memories attached to these.

He offered the young couple some and they gladly took one each and then munched on the sweets.

Looking up, Molly caught Adam's knowing look. "Crossing so many lines." She tried to keep the words low.

"Right up my alley, wouldn't you say?"

The way he dropped his gaze to her lips made them tingle. Heat crawled up her neck. "Now." She cleared her throat. "Kyra—"

Molly halted at the covert looks passing between the couple. "What? We're…friends. He likes being a pest, don't you, Adam?"

"Friends? Really, Moll?" He looked hurt. "It's only been recent and she forgets. Quickly."

Her breath tumbled behind her rib cage. The lies were piling up and she was having a difficult time keeping track of them, especially with Adam so close. What was real anymore? "Business…partners."

"Yes, the barn, too!" Kyra clasped her hands to her chest. "I can't wait to see it all made up and fancy."

"Yeah, too bad we didn't know or we would have saved for it and booked it." Kyle gave his fiancée a shrug. "We'll go with the backyard reception at your folks' place."

Adam leaned in, sorting through the mocked up save the date cards. "Hold up. We open first weekend in June. Yours isn't until the fourth. I don't recall filling that date yet. Why not?"

Molly jerked her head to look at his dead sober expression. Kyle and Kyra must have, too; the way Adam glanced at them and back at Molly. "Seriously, Adam?" She couldn't seem to find the right words, or enough of them, at the moment, so caught up in the rumbling anticipation.

He swept her face with a thorough, intense gaze before settling on her eyes. "Kyle and Kyra, what about that modeling work I mentioned? We can call it an even trade. And only with your help, Moll. You and I can pull this off. Together."

The air swirled with bubbling tension. Adam wanted more from her and not just for this one event. The pressure mounted. Did she dare go all in? Did she dare make this a semipublic announcement that she was on board with the entire charade?

Breaking the undeniable tug of awareness, Molly sucked in a shaky breath. She turned to a hopeful Kyle and Kyra, waiting with bated breaths, so much like Adam and she had been years ago—young, on the cusp of a new and scary future, and head over heels in love.

Could they rewrite their own broken history with this couple?

Chapter Eleven

"YOU'RE STILL HERE." Molly moved with precision and determination at her desk. Between the computer and light box, she continued to work, in spite of her shaky hands and Adam's looming presence circling her shop and then back again. He eyed her large poster-like photos and then rearranged them at an angle.

Of course, they did look better that way. But she wasn't about to let him know that.

It had been nearly two hours since she'd agreed to be a reluctant participant in his venture.

Kyle's and Kyra's squeals still echoed in Molly's head, the fierce hugs might have crushed a rib bone or two. Thankfully, they'd chosen the shots for the save the date card, others for family and friends, and some for them before they rushed out the door, unable to contain the news from their parents any longer. Okay, Kyra more than Kyle.

Years ago, Molly recalled that heady thrill and overwhelming excitement. Now, not so much.

Especially as wedding after wedding loomed in her future.

Fake reunion with Adam? *Yeah, that's a hard no.*

I must be a hundred points down by now. It's bad enough I'm thrown into the thick of someone else's love story, with icing on top, but to melt over all those hot looks he'd sent my way...

The first ceremony and reception would be their trial mockup one, or, better terminology, a publicity event to look like the dream wedding each couple, wedding coordinator or planner, would expect at the venue. Each one after, they'd perfect the flaws and improve on the wins. Oh, great!

Surrounded by happy couples and their exquisite plans...

What have I gotten myself into?

I'm supposed to be recovering from all this.

Cold turkey. Yeah, not.

More times than not, Adam was on his cell phone, asking her for some paper and a pen, taking notes, and chewing on the licorice absently as he held conversation after conversation for his business. Every once in a while, he'd unthinkingly wave the red stick around for emphasis.

Gosh, he's breathtaking!

That look—focused, intent, searing when directed at her—proved disconcerting. Or was that her equilibrium disrupted? *Well, definitely disturbed, for sure.*

"Focus, Molly." She kept her tone low. Going back to the images, she grinned. The triplets, in various unguarded poses in their costumes, filled the screen. Each one made Molly smile more. She giggled at their silly faces.

In the back of her mind, she noted footsteps drawing close. "What's that?"

She jumped at Adam's voice near her ear. "You could

warn a person, Larson."

"Hey, they're adorable." He pointed to the screen and then to several strips of images on her light box.

"The sisters or the pics?" She had no doubt he meant the lively trio.

Adam picked up her magnifying piece—spyglass, as she called it—and leaned over her shoulder.

He was a hairsbreadth away. His warm, clean scent plunged her senses into overdrive. She recalled him holding her close as they danced at high school prom and the sweep of heat and wonder nearly overcoming her at how magnificent he felt and smelled then.

Better with age! How does he do that?

Swallowing hard, she remembered his soft kisses and how he tasted of that red licorice or peppermints.

"You're amazing." His words of praise sprinkled over her, making her blood spark and shoot flares of want and need through her.

Molly tried to shake it off. Or was it this glowing inside her? "It's them. Not me."

"No way. Look. This one, she's definitely the leader. Kinda bossy and brash. She is going to rule her world."

Grinning, Molly agreed. "How could you tell?"

"You captured it here and there. This one, she's the girly girl. Glitter and sparkles."

She marveled at his perception. "And this one?" She longed to hear what he had to say.

"The pleaser. Middle one, right? She goes back and forth. Part tomboy, too, by the basketball she's got pinned under one foot."

"Dead on, Adam."

"No, you are. You made them shine." He flipped to another row. "See the traditional ones are boring and bland. You can't even tell them apart. No personality coming through. Not your fault, though, it's too pristine and proper."

It was actually what she'd thought at the time. "That part nearly put me to sleep. Well, except for the racket they were making, whining and complaining." She gulped. "Their poor mom, not a good look on a young woman."

"You're incredibly talented."

"Heaping on the praise? No need. I've signed on already, remember?" There, she'd admitted it out in the open.

"Still can't take a compliment. Especially on your work." He sized her up. Again.

"Hollow?" At his wince of pain, she held up her hand. "Unfair. Sorry. But I don't believe I do anything special."

"What the—" He pulled himself up short, stepped back, and then eyed her closely. "Molly, really? Stop kidding yourself. No, stop selling yourself short."

That dropped between them, hard and heavy.

It stunned her speechless; he was serious with a hint of angry.

The well of frustration radiating from him caused her to blink and shake her head. "You can't be—" It came out on a squeak.

The tight swell in the air between them pushed invisible walls, barely holding in place.

"You were always short-changing yourself back then. I couldn't let you give this up for an ordinary life with me. Not then. You major in teaching instead of a bachelor in arts or photography because you could get a better job after college?"

She recalled the blunted edge of regret when she'd made that call. Like her parents said, she had to be realistic about life and get a real job, one that paid. *Because who knew if Adam could provide for her.* The words tumbled through her mind now and grabbed ahold of her throat. They'd been against the young marriage—subtly planting doubts in her all along.

With that, what Adam had told her now, and about the money talk with her father, Molly understood so much more.

"Protect Molly, right? Because I lived in my heart—with hopes and dreams—not in my head—in the real world." The strain in her voice echoed the ache in her chest.

Everyone longed to take care of her as if she were some weak, fragile shell of a person ready to crack at any minute.

The preemie baby they'd almost lost, the little child who had failed and had to repeat kindergarten, of all things. So her parents moved the family to Cupid's Corner to make life easier for her, the layer of invisible gauze wrapped around her all through the years, the excuses her parents made for her or the silent warnings they'd sent out to others like a radar to treat her gently and with care, and the way she'd been handled delicately and fussed over…

Adam clamped his jaw tight, the muscle along it jumping.

It told her a great deal.

The jangle over the door shattered the tension and brought a whirl of activity in the form of the triplets. Their weary mom followed at a much slower pace.

Molly released her pent-up breath, needing the distraction from her whirling thoughts and painful emotions.

It wasn't every day a girl discovered how little her family imagined she was capable of and how her one-time fiancé walked away, maybe to toughen her up a bit.

Deep down, the blistering wounds bubbled, on the edge of spilling over.

There was something else gathering along her spine. A steely backbone, perhaps?

THANKFULLY FOR MOLLY and the triplets' mom, Robin Henderson, while discussing images and photo packages, Adam took charge of the overzealous trio.

"He's a wonder with them." Their mom glanced over more than once to capture a silly antic as they practically took over the shop, careful of her expensive equipment.

"Yeah, who knew red licorice sticks could be lady bug antennas, a fake mustache, or even woven into a haphazard tiara?" She marveled at Adam's ability to entertain—no, to care so dang much about giving the girls a lively distraction and enjoy it at the same time.

A tug or half a dozen yanked behind her rib cage. The

thought of what if they'd had kids together and what type of father he'd have been simmered through her like a warm, delicious ache. He'd have been a great one...

Molly didn't recall hearing Adam laugh so much before. And the girls' giggles were like music floating in the air.

The girls came up behind her, fitting a white tulle wedding veil on top of her ponytail, with Adam directing them.

She felt for it, going to take it out, and then stopped at the crestfallen looks on all four of their faces.

"For my bride." Adam's voice caught.

Jules rose up, practically standing on her tippy toes. "Can we be the flower girls, Adam. Pretty please?" Soon her sisters joined in.

Adam gave them a half smile, half frown look that tugged hard and sharp inside Molly. "Silly. Who else could do the job, but you three?"

They jumped with joy and hollered with ear-splitting squeals.

"That's a yes then." Adam spread his arms and grinned at Molly as he backed up to play groom—accepting the top hat from the girls.

"I'm sold. On you two and the pictures." Robin tapped the stack of fun, spirited shots of the triplets in their costumes. "You were right." She held them up side by side to the tame, sedate ones and compared. A sweet smile crossed her lips. "Years from now, when I look back, I want to look at these and see their adorable personalities." She drew in a heavy breath. "I need to see them like this more, so I don't lose them in all the frantic day-to-day duties. Anymore."

Somehow, Molly sensed the struggle. "I don't know how you do it all. But, really, they're great. Just a tad rambunctious all put together."

As they both turned to see Adam teach the girls how to walk down a pretend aisle, holding imaginary baskets, and tossing out invisible rose petals, their mother sighed. "He's great with them. Their dad? Too busy working long, grueling hours at two jobs so we can buy that new house." She swallowed hard, blinking back the sudden moisture in her eyes. "He's missing out. We all are in a way. Family time? That's nonexistent. I think that's why the girls are such a handful lately, too."

Molly reached out and touched the back of Robin's hand, offering what little comfort she could. "Tell him."

"I will if you will." She countered with a half smile and a nod to Adam.

Slowly, Molly withdrew, taking back her hand and curling her fingers against the woodgrain on the tabletop. "What could I possible have to tell him?"

"Oh, I don't know. Maybe it's the way you look at him with such longing. Or the way he glances at you now and then. There's something real there. I remember those exchanges I had with my hubby before the kids." She sighed. "You know, the rumors are swirling."

"More?" It couldn't possibly have spread that fast that soon.

Molly tried to chuckle, but it came out raw and strangled. She hated being the object of someone else's conversation.

"Small-town life. It's only bad when they're talking about you. And I've heard plenty about me. 'Why did she go and have all those kids at once?' Yeah, like I had a choice in the matter." For the first time, she laughed without restraint, the frazzled look gone for once. "Of course, my husband had nothing to do with it at all."

Molly joined in her laughter. "Men. They get off scot-free."

But Adam hadn't. Not when he'd first left and even now when the townspeople shot him a glare.

"I'd better go."

"Discount price." Molly grinned. "Frames included in the package deal, remember?"

Robin wrote out the check, ripped it from the book, and then handed it over. "Their grandmothers are going to love the Mother's Day gifts. Perfect. And I don't have to go shopping."

"Thanks." Emboldened by her current successful attempt at pushing against the tried and true, Molly gathered up her courage. "Ah, would you mind if I enlarged a few of these and put them in the shop window on display?" Molly shrugged awkwardly. She'd love to keep doing sessions like that one—creative and artistic and inspiring. "To show people they have new options for poses and pictures."

"Why not? The girls will love seeing them when we stroll through town."

A few minutes later, with Adam by Molly's side—so close she could feel his body heat—they waved off the sweet little family, echoing promises of seeing them soon.

"Don't forget, Mr. Adam, you said you'd ask our daddy for us."

"Of course." To Molly, he whispered under his breath, "The boss lady."

She giggled at the accurate observation. "What are you asking anyway?" With her senses heightened being around him, Molly went to the table to straighten up the remaining pictures into a pile, picking them up, and tapping the bottom against the table to get them all in line before she filed them away.

"A play house."

When she jerked to look at him, he had the good grace to wince.

"They twisted my arm. How was I going to get out of it?"

"Pushover." But something unfurled inside of Molly. A ray of promise.

He returned her smile, slow and sexy, and her heart jolted clear to her throat.

Somehow, in spite of her best efforts, the hopeless romantic longed to burst out.

Recovering, my patootie!

Down, girl! We can't get twisted up and torn apart all over again. Because seeing him today with the adorable little girls made Molly ache to her bones. He would have been a really incredible father to their kids.

And a caring, loving man to her.

That was the past, or what could have been. But that was never going to happen. She couldn't catch lightning in a bottle twice in one lifetime, right?

Chapter Twelve

"LUNCH? I'M STARVING." Adam joined Molly on the sidewalk, waiting for her to lock up her shop. He nodded across and down the street. "The new Italian place again?"

There was a small crowd forming a line outside. That meant lots of locals. His belly clenched and not from hunger pangs.

"Ah, no. And get raked over the coals?" Molly shivered. "I hate to tell you this, Larson, but I understand the dear people of Cupid's Corner are speculating about us."

Even more so now.

Weary defeat translated to her leaden steps as she barely kept up with his strides. Adam slowed, mulling over what she'd said. "We could give them something to talk about right here."

"No!" She smacked his arm. Her ever present camera around her neck shifted and swung with the movement. "Not on your life. You'll leave and I'll be stuck with those oh-poor-Molly looks. Again."

That made his heart twist. He'd never known. Somehow

he only thought she'd benefit all around in the end from his disappearing act. Her life hadn't been as wonderful without him as he'd imagined.

He tried to tease her to make them both feel better. "Oh, a little temper from my red-headed angel." He half grinned at her, enjoying the flush creeping up her neck.

However, in the back of his mind, he duly noted her transparent remarks. So, they'd been sharp-eyed and maybe sharp-tongued, most likely about him.

It wasn't anything he wasn't used to growing up here on the wrong side of the tracks. *Why disappoint their low expectations, right?* People had a way of telling him what they thought of him and his family even without words. Just a look or a lifted eyebrow spoke volumes. Most days, he let it slide off his shoulders. Of course, they'd cheered him when he played running back on the high school football team and scored lots of touchdowns.

The more he'd won, the less they pointed out his and his family's lack of wealth. That was certainly a good incentive back then.

Adam halted at the town parking spot when Molly pivoted to face the corner. "Where are we going?"

"Come on, slow poke. There's traffic down there coming our way." She snagged his hand and dragged him across the for now empty street.

Her hand was so small in his big one and cold, too. Her fingers were like ice. But the innocent touch sparked nerves and flares up his arm, reminding him of their long ago past.

What he'd lost by walking away…

The pain rocked him all the way to his toes. It didn't help that meeting the triplets had put thoughts of kids—Molly and his—in his head.

"You all right, Larson? It's just a few streets over on Maple."

"Sure." He refused to let go of her hand as they strolled past the ice cream shop and old movie theater.

"Do you mind?" She tried to tug it free.

"Yes, I do. You're freezing. Where's your jacket?"

"Where's yours?"

"Testy?"

Molly halted, turning to face him, still attempting to take her hand away.

Her blue eyes glittered with determination and something else he couldn't quite make out. "I'm not your project, all right? I realize most people consider me weak and—"

"And what?"

"Fragile. Heartbroken." Her voice cracked.

Gut punch. He sucked in a sharp breath. Her protest defied the shadows crossing her gorgeous eyes.

"If you say so." His words were soft and tender as they scraped up from his throat and out of his mouth.

She squeezed her eyes shut for a moment and then gazed back up at him. "You don't play fair, Larson. I'm trying to adult here."

"Is it working?"

"Fat chance."

"Look, angel, you don't have to pretend with me. You never did before. You don't have to now. I get it. You're petite and shy and use your camera to keep the world at a distance and your folks put you in a category and never let you out." The stark truth of that hit him square in his chest. "Me, too."

"Adam." She gripped his hand tight.

He clung to it, not just for the warmth spreading, but the connection to her. "No one expected us to be more than they pigeon-holed us into."

"You included." Awe and wonder chased across her features. "*We* didn't even trust us to be more, to be better."

"Fooled them, didn't we?" It hurt to talk, to rip away the layers of rock and cement and allow the truth to bubble up inside him. He'd played into the lies.

Deep inside, he wondered if he'd asked her to wait if that would have changed their outcome. Would she have said yes to that?

He'd never know.

Maybe he didn't want to know.

Dreams weren't meant to come true in love or life, not for him, were they? Or was that all another lie he'd bought into back then and wouldn't let go of even now...

THERE WAS SOMETHING raw and new between them now as Adam held open the door to Between Two Slices for Molly to enter ahead of him. She was dainty and perfect, with a trace of floral perfume lingering as she drew near and surpassed him.

"Have I got a treat for you." She grinned.

It didn't quite mask the pain in her glance, but it gave him hope she'd recover from their encounter—in the past and now. *Heal her deep inside.*

It's the least he could do for her.

The only thing, other than rising out of her financial circumstances, he could offer her now.

His mind raced with thoughts and questions as to why not more.

The heavenly scent of freshly baked bread assaulted his senses the moment he walked in behind her. It was a classic one-counter sandwich shop with a few scattered tables in front.

However, the long variety of selections etched in chalk hanging on the wall behind the register spoke of innovation and daring mouthwatering adventures.

There were two people in line and a group of four men nearby, eating gigantic heapings of meat, cheese, and lettuce stuffed between thick layers of bread like that guy in the comic strip his dad used to read to Adam and his mom.

"Wait for it…" Molly smiled full on.

The power of that look directed at him nearly knocked Adam into yesterday.

To say he was dazzled would be an understatement. "Ah, for what?" He shook his head, feeling like he'd just woken up from a concussion—the last one being in a high school football game.

"Geez." She pointed a finger, counting under her breath. "Seven down on the right. Under New England specialties."

Quickly, Adam followed her directions, skipping over the fried baloney and then he screeched to a halt. "Whoa! No way. Deep-fried fluffernutter! Tell me I'm dreaming. No, don't. If this is a dream I don't want to wake up." He chuckled. "Is it good? It's got to be, right?"

"Would I lead you astray?" She held up a hand. "Don't answer that one."

"I haven't had a fluffernutter in ages."

"How could you not? It's only your favorite in the whole wide world."

They laughed together, recalling his everyday sandwich of choice for lunch. For once, it hadn't been about money. It had been about the taste.

Adam rubbed his hands together. "So, what are you getting?"

"Drop down one." She teased him with a flirty look.

"They didn't. Deep-fried chocolatefluff sandwich."

"Yep. Delish. If you're very nice, I'll even let you try a bit."

"Tempting." But he wasn't talking about the new flavor. No, Adam was looking at her mouth. The soft, sweet lips he hadn't ever gotten enough of back in the day and wasn't likely to ever have the chance again. But a guy could dream about that at least…

Heat gathered low and deep.

She must have sensed the shift in him; she elbowed him in the arm. "Quit that."

Adam chuckled. She'd done that in school, too. "No, you quit it. Stop looking so good, angel."

Right on cue, the flush crawled up her neck.

Some things never changed, in a good way.

At the moment, he didn't want to be anywhere else or with anyone else. Tiny sparks ignited in his veins, traveling through his bloodstream.

Yeah, some things never change.

MOLLY EYED ADAM as they slid onto opposite seats at the square table on the small wooden deck overlooking the pond at the back of Between Two Slices.

The slight breeze ruffled his short hair. The afternoon sun warmed the chilly places inside her. Or was that from Adam and the covert stares he'd shoot her way every now and then?

He's here. So very close. And it felt so good to hold his warm, strong hand again.

"Ready?" She set their tall milk with a heavy dose of coffee syrup added aside and then nudged his plate toward him. "Try it and tell me what you think?"

She held her breath, hoping he'd like the new version of his old favorite. There was something special in sharing this simple pleasure with him. *Delight? Anticipation?* That could be said about Adam himself.

"Here goes." He managed to wrangle the warm, overflowing sandwich and lift it to his mouth. He sank his teeth in and moaned.

Adam closed his eyes and chewed slowly, savoring it.

"Okay. I'm sold. Last meal."

Molly giggled at their old game of declaring what they'd want for their last meal ever. "That's saying something. But you haven't tried this one yet." She took a bit from the corner. Chocolate spread, fluff, and warm bread melted on her tongue. "Heaven."

"So delicate." He made a sound in the back of his throat.

"Your turn." She held it for him and he took a large bite.

"Dang, that's great! Just needs peanut butter and it's moving quickly up the charts."

She grinned. "They have that way, too."

"Next time we're here that's what I'll get then."

Something warm and wonderful sparkled through her. She liked this Adam—open and freer.

Molly tried to break his captivating stare. "So, uh, what's on the agenda next? For the barn that is?"

"The cleanup has been a bear to contend with. That violent windstorm did more damage than we first thought—the roof, of course, but the way it crumbled in and took out the top loft and some pretty important beams. The entire structure has to be shored up from the bottom up." He nodded across the pond and high up the hill to the barn—only the tip of it visible from this angle—while he continued to eat.

From this side, it seemed the same, partially hidden by overgrown trees and dripping branches. However, on the other side, there were dozens of trucks and workers engaged in getting the job done right. If she hadn't picked up on anything in the hours she photographed the place, she'd discovered Adam received a great deal of respect and dedication from his employees.

"I'm headed back after lunch to pitch in." He wiped his hands on a white napkin.

Yeah, and he didn't ask anything of his people that he wouldn't do himself. Pride beamed inside her for him and all he'd accomplished. His very own company in less than six short years. That was amazing.

A niggling truth pinched her belly. He wouldn't have accomplished that with her in his life as his wife. No, he'd have played it safe, not stretching or growing because he'd worried about giving her a secure life and future instead of putting them in jeopardy time after time.

No risk. No chances. No way out of the box.

For the first time, Molly really looked long and hard at what they'd been up against. She'd have gone into teaching or something equally as boring to her just to contribute to their household. Her photography would have lagged way behind.

They would have survived, but not thrived in what they were both meant to do.

It would have taken ten, fifteen, even twenty years to get to the point they were both at now, if they wanted a stable environment for themselves and any kids they'd have had.

Kids. Her stomach quivered at the thought. First, of having Adam's children. *That would have been incredible.* Then of struggling to keep it all together.

Her parents, Adam's parents, and even their friends had been right. *We were too young then. Misinformed, too, or just plain fanciful on my part.*

She especially had brushed aside their concerns and vowed to do whatever she had to in order to make it work.

"Hey, you all right?" Adam frowned, getting up and sliding into the seat beside her, brushing her knee by accident. He reached over and, with the pad of his thumb, wiped the corner of her mouth and then brought it to his and licked it. "Marshmallow."

The simple, tender gesture—the slight roughness of his skin—rippled through her on a far more intimate level.

Underneath it all, they were still Adam and Molly. She swallowed hard.

Molly sucked in a sharp, quivery breath. She'd lost her appetite for food, but wanted more of Adam. "So, after the structure comes together, what then?"

"Replacing the caved-in parts and then redoing the floor with reclaimed boards. In the meantime, we can work on our first wedding at the barn." He raised his eyebrows at her groan. "Tsk. Tsk. You might have me thinking you're against the publicity it will bring or something. Look, we have the place—spotlighting our creation together—and now the flower girls. Two down. Okay, four. We can check off bride and groom from the long list. Progress."

"Or not." She sipped her coffee milk loudly, rolling her eyes at him.

"Should I get a wedding planner then?"

"No." She shook her head. The least amount of people involved in a hint of a charade the better. It was bad enough he was pushing for a fake reunion. "It's not ours. We're not a couple. There is no fake *anything*, got it?" How many times did she have to drum it into his head?

"Ideal wedding? Hmm…let's see if I remember." He stared off across the pond, the corners of his lips lifting.

Oh, not the look that makes my insides tumble.

"Rustic but chic, isn't that what you said? With lots of lilacs. Your favorites."

Molly gulped hard, air squeezing out of her throat so she could barely breathe. He hadn't forgotten, especially her flower.

"Nothing." He waved a hand in front of her face. "All right then." He wiped his hands on his white napkin. "I'll take over. I'll work on ordering the supplies for the interior. Lots of antler chandeliers—"

She jerked her head back, unable to remain silent with that hideous choice. *Not at my wedding.* "Wait. What? This isn't a hunting lodge we're talking about."

"But it's rustic." He looked pained and confused. "With the interior covered in white paint it won't look so hunter-ish."

"Wh-white paint?" She nearly hyperventilated. *How awful to cover that beautiful wood.*

"Whitewash everything. Clean, fresh look."

"The walls? The floors?"

"Sure, why not?"

"No. I mean, you can't possibly do that." Her voice rose an octave.

He truly looked baffled.

"Adam, you can't. It will look modern farmhouse—cute,

but not for this project—and not rustic chic."

"What's the difference? Isn't it one and the same, just with different names?"

Molly groaned at the injustice. "Have you gone mad, Larson? No, don't answer. Obviously, you need—"

"Help. Yes, exactly!" He snapped his fingers. "That's it. I'll take you up on your generous offer."

Her chuckle came out weak and on a puff of air. "Think again."

"I just did. It's perfect. You're the expert."

"Not in the least."

"Well, you know more than I do."

"That's a given." She poked fun at him and enjoyed his grin at that.

"You love weddings, Moll. Come on. I have some frou-frou interior designer from the city who suggested the all-white look, so save me from colossal mistakes. I've got connections with suppliers, home decor, light fixture places, dishes and things…" He shook his head. "Yeah, I'm no good at this girly stuff. Guy stuff." He held out his hand and tilted it back and forth. "So-so."

If her insides weren't all shivery and quivery before from being so close to Adam, they certainly were now with his tempting suggestion.

You're recovering, remember? "I—I have so much…many pictures to take."

"Of course, that comes first. I saw your schedule on your desk littered with proms, reunions, anniversaries… Hmm, surprisingly few weddings."

Her heart jolted. "I'm working on them." She couldn't give him any more telling information. "There's room to grow."

"That's it, Moll. This would be an amazing chance for you. Not only with documenting the renovations, but putting *your* stamp on this venue."

Adam leaned in, his eyes captured her gaze. His were hypnotic and excitement danced in them.

"Honestly, angel." His voice cracked. "I want you there by my side. Us creating something beautiful and lasting for Cupid's Corner."

His soft words fluttered through her, teasing like butterfly wings. "Memorable." *Did he have her in a trance?*

"You lived and breathed weddings our senior year. All those ideas you had, even ones we decided not to do for our own. Don't let them go to waste."

"Persuasion powers?"

He chuckled. The rich, beautiful sound radiated inside her. "Say yes then."

Thousands of reasons why not ricocheted in her mind. All of them were dismissed when a big, overriding one took hold.

Here's my chance to show everyone I'm not that young woman anymore who lived on only fantasy and escape. What better way to show them I'm truly over and done with dreamland by treating this like a job and, when all was over, coming out of this wedding venture unscathed and solidly on my own two feet again.

Keep it up. I may end up believing it myself.

Molly gulped. *Yeah, first show myself I can brush it off, because I'm drooling at images clicking in my head.*

"Everything you always wanted, Molly."

It was there. He dangled it in front of her like the sweetest treat for a hopeless romantic, except she wasn't one anymore. *Are, too. Am not! My dream wedding...*

"No expense spared."

"My payback?"

"I give you what you want." His tone grew husky. "And you give me what I want. We both win here, angel."

"Everything on the line." *Including my dignity, worse, my heart.* What will he lose himself? Because they would both pay a price for this.

"How much is this worth to you, Larson?"

Chapter Thirteen

ADAM SENSED THE definite shift in Molly. Reluctance gave way to full speed ahead.

Days flew by into weeks as Molly took control of the interior renovations. Along with business shoots and her photographing their progress—in the adorable pink hardhat he'd gotten for her—she'd peppered him with dozens of questions. Mostly, she gathered info on how he intended to use the place in addition to weddings, took copious notes, made rudimentary drawings, and reveled in the plans.

He'd always thought of her as adorable, but now she was glowing and more beautiful than he ever recalled. To put it mildly, she stole his breath away. It wasn't just the way she came to life. Her joy radiated, touching everyone nearby—especially him.

She'd given her input on events and expanded his narrow thinking and limitations on celebrations. There was so much more they could tap into. Her vision energized him.

This was a Cupid's Corner landmark and she urged him to see it in that very light. A Valentine's Day dance for starters.

Yep, missed that obvious one.

He marveled at her enthusiasm and delight. Even the smallest detail was addressed, down to handles and lanterns and gravel type. Who knew?

Now, he stood on the bank of the pond, waiting for her. There was something about the calmness of the water and the heady scent of freshly rained on grass that opened all his senses. Or maybe it was just being around his Molly again…

"Hello, we have a meeting, remember?" she called from behind and above him.

Adam turned and, in midgrin, his breath got sucked out of his lungs, fast and sharp. She was standing in the opening of the second-floor carriage house where the doors slid back and the new windows he'd put in fully spread open.

That was his domain now. He'd claimed it and made it his temporary home. To think she so easily fit there. Wicked thoughts scattered through his imagination.

Male appreciation sent a powerful surge through his bloodstream.

Seeing her—red hair loose down her back and with the breeze teasing it, skinny jeans, tucked-in scooped, long-sleeved slate-blue T-shirt—made him weak in the knees.

"Well, what do you have to say for yourself?"

"I wish—" Adam stopped short.

He tugged out his cell phone from his back pocket and quickly took three pictures, trying to get the best angle. He should have taken lessons from her all those years ago.

She giggled. "Really? I'm a mess, Larson." She dragged a hand through her tousled hair, with her face turned slightly up to the sun, and her eyes half closed.

Wow! Something coiled tighter inside him. He snapped another shot, liking this one the most. She had no clue how sensually she moved, yet stayed sweet and innocent.

In high school, she'd brushed off his compliments. Her shy ways overwhelmed her underlying grace.

But here it was.

"Are you done?"

Not by a long shot.

Adam wasn't talking pictures, either. His insides tumbled, like he'd fallen off a twenty-foot-high roof and didn't know where or if he'd land on his feet ever again.

"Come on down, Moll!" His parched throat barely worked. "Business meeting on the pond."

She hesitated for a moment, slid the windows shut, and then disappeared.

With his heartbeat hammering away—*thug, thug*—he watched and waited. Finally, she appeared, walking alongside the carriage house and to the hilltop. She held her camera by the short strap and began the descent to where he stood.

Sure-footed on the slick, damp grass, she reached him in no time, stopping to face him.

"You didn't say anything about a hike first. Or a boat ride." She swallowed hard.

Her blue eyes clouded. "Business, really? It seems more like going down memory lane to me."

Guilt warred inside Adam, along with remorse and longing, topping it all off like a cherry on a hot fudge sundae.

People weren't just talking. No, Molly and his reunion

made *Cupid's Corner Gazette*, along with the continuing progress of their venture. Everywhere they went, they were watched and whispered about—even among his loyal crew. Speculation grew with the sightings and copious wedding items ordered or detailed in another telling article.

How could he do this to her? Bring her back to their special place and pressure her into working for him on the wedding venue? She was creating an opening event, not anything near their supposed wedding, as the gazette alluded to.

But worse, how could he even pretend this afternoon wasn't about them? The urge to re-create the boat ride where he'd proposed to her years ago couldn't be denied.

"Nothing will happen that you don't want to." That was about as neutral as Adam could give her. In the back of his mind, he hoped he soothed his own troubled conscience. Deep down, he battled with the past and the present. "Afraid?"

"Of you? As if," she bit back, jamming her hands on her hips.

He grinned. "Yourself, Moll. Afraid we could just step on back to what we had?" That spoke more along the lines of what he'd been dreaming of at night lately.

He'd woken up many a morning confused and yet wishing things he shouldn't.

She bristled. "Is this some kind of game? Because I am not playing it. What's this all about, Adam?"

God help him, but he really liked this new Molly— fierce, emboldened, take no prisoners, and giving him attitude. His equal in every way.

"Advertising shots. Getting a wider angle and the pond view. Hopefully, before more rain rolls in." He tipped his head toward the small dock with old man Pickens's wooden boat tied up. "I tried a camera drone, but it didn't do some areas justice. Not like you can."

The bottled-up air siphoned out of her. "Oh."

"That's not to say, I wouldn't turn away a kiss or two."

She smacked his arm. "Fat chance, Larson."

Adam chuckled, adoring the way her snapping blue eyes fired from within. "So, I take that as a no. But if you change your mind…"

"Let's just go already." She marched off with heavy footsteps.

"Eager, too." Adam followed close behind as he pocketed his phone.

"Don't push your luck."

"What? Don't you miss what we had, Moll?" Where did those words come from? They zinged him as hard as they appeared to have her, by the way she snapped a jerky glance at him.

She remained silent as she looped the camera strap around her neck, carefully held on to the chunky wood post at the end of the dock, and then gingerly stepped into the small boat.

Molly took the seat—a lone board across the width—in the front.

Misty rain began and Adam wondered if he should call it off. Something urged him on. He tried to dismiss the desire to spend more alone time with Molly. But it tugged at him.

He untied the thick rope, tossed it in the boat, and then hopped on to take the back seat. *Just like old times.*

Grabbing the oars, Adam set to work—shoving one against the sun-bleached dock to get them started. The old familiar creaking sounds of shifting the wooden oars in their metal holdings and then dipping them in the water rushed back to him.

With some effort, he steered the small two-person boat around and pointed it in the right direction, now easing up on the rowing.

"Do you?" Her stark words dropped into the hushed air.

Adam went back to his last question and mulled over his answer for a few moments. "I stayed away from Cupid's Corner for a long time. I finally figured out that the haunting memories were there, no matter if I was here or not." He caught and held her gaze. "I keep seeing you. How shattered you looked." He cleared his throat. "I never meant to hurt you."

"You did, Adam." She brushed away a tear. Clutching her camera, she brought it to her eye, focused it, and then snapped pictures.

He ached all the way down to his bones. "I'm sorry, Moll."

"That's the second time you've said that." She heaved out a breath. "Make it three if you include that day."

"I meant it then just like I do now." He focused on the physical activity, rowing and holding steady, hugging the boat close to shore for her for a few images and then gliding the oars in the water away for a longer, wider angle. "I couldn't give you what you needed."

"Strange, I wanted you."

"There's a difference, you know. Needing versus wanting. Sure, we could have got the wanting part easily. Heck, we had that down." He tried to laugh, but it came out raw and rough, tearing him apart inside.

Molly turned to him, with the camera shielding her, as she took a picture of him. "Tell me."

"With that thing to hide you?" He grimaced.

"It...shows me if a person is being genuine." The words came out slow and tortured.

Shock reverberated through Adam. "Trust?" She didn't trust him to tell her the truth? That stung deep in his chest.

"I see things better." Still she kept it between them.

A ripple of anger rolled through his gut. "All right, Molly McCleary." He halted, securing the oars, and then leaned in closer, so close he could hear her tiny gasp and feel her sweet breath fan his mouth. He wanted to shake her and kiss her.

Adam held tight to his warring emotions. "See this, why don't you?" Adam drew in a short, painful breath. "I was crazy about you—every little thing—from the shy looks under your long, dark spiky lashes, to that hint of a smile tugging up your luscious lips, to the way you held me up on that invisible pedestal, to your sweet laugh, to your hopes and dreams for us, to spending hours getting the perfect shot of me or anything, helping other kids with their homework so they could pass, how funny and silly you were with Gemma, and more so with me, how caring and loving your heart was. You made me feel like a giant. Feel special, just for being me. No one had ever done that before."

Her hands shook and the camera slipped down a notch.

If he hadn't have guessed it before, Adam did now. "No one has ever done it since, Molly." No one ever loved him like she had.

And he never loved anyone like he had her. *Still do.*

I love this woman!

She owns my heart. Still.

Molly dropped the camera—it jerked to a halt at the end of the strap before it could hit her lap.

Her wide eyes searched his intent gaze. "Ad-am?"

"Yeah, that." His words were fierce and clipped.

"Still?"

"Crazy, isn't it?"

"You're confused."

"Am I?" He watched the war chasing across her features, fighting with the knowledge.

"It's the past…"

"I'm right here in the present, angel."

Molly lifted her hand, tenderly touching his cheek and then brushing her fingertips over his lips, outlining them. "I shouldn't want this."

"But there's a part that does."

"Do you always have to have the last word, Adam?" But there was a longing deep in her gorgeous blue eyes and a slight crack in her voice.

Chapter Fourteen

S TUNNED WONDER TUMBLED inside Molly. Her mind registered his words, but her heart thumped wildly in her chest.

It can't be.

He'd mixed things up. Hadn't he?

For the first time, she put down her camera—her shield and truth teller—to really, truly gaze into his beautiful green eyes filled with…

No, I can't go there.

By slow degrees, as if time stood still, Molly leaned forward. She brushed her fingertips down to touch the barely there stubble on his chin. She lowered her gaze the moment before she touched her lips to his.

Soft. Sweet.

Molly sighed.

He shivered.

She'd waited years to kiss him again. Years filled with loss and yearning.

They seemed to come out now in her as she lingered and brushed hers against his. Warm. Firm. Tantalizing. She'd never initiated this before, never imagined she could ask for what she wanted—with him. Or anyone else in her life. He must have sensed the fresh wave of hesitancy.

"Don't stop." His voice, raw and rough, did the strangest things to her insides.

"We only have now. Savor it." She shook her head, sounding incoherent to own ears.

However, she kissed him again, gently drawing out the sweetness as she melted at his tenderness. His hand brushed back her hair, now getting wetter as the rain came down. The cool rivulets plopped down her back.

Molly became aware of her surroundings. *What am I doing?* Shock at her boldness—at kissing Adam again—caused her to jerk away and back.

The boat rocked.

She gripped the edges as it swayed one way and then the other.

Adam, looking stunned, lurched for the oar tilting on the edge. He knocked it off instead. It splashed into the water. He lunged for it, his hand skimming it, and then accidentally shoving the oar farther away.

"Hold on! I'm going after it." Standing awkwardly, he half fell, half jumped into the pond.

The *thunk* of him landing in the water—the cold spray hitting Molly—and then the *glunk-glunk* of his going under jerked her out of her hazy stupor.

Molly wished the boat would stop reeling, but she scrambled around to see Adam break the surface with the oar outstretched in his arm, while moving his other in the water to stay afloat.

"Got it!"

She giggled at his outrageously triumphant stance, like some god rising from the depths with his prize. Molly dragged her strap off her neck and secured her precious camera in the bottom of the boat. She steadied her knees and reached out. "Give me your hand."

Instead, Adam gave her the oar.

She tucked it back in its nest and returned to find him peering over the rim at her. "Care to join me?"

"No, silly. It must be freezing." She wiggled her fingers for him to take.

"Best if you hold on to the other side. Counterweight it. I'll try not to tip it when I hoist myself up."

Before she could react, he'd already attempted to drag himself over the edge. She squealed and then slid to the far side, anchoring her arms and her feet. It worked, because the boat jerked, but didn't flip as he yanked himself over and half rolled in—splayed across the seats.

"Adam?" She remained where she was, gritting her teeth at the bobbing sensation.

He looked up at the gray sky, with rain coming down on his face, and then he laughed. He reached out for her.

Molly allowed him to tug her close and nestle her head on his shoulder as they both looked up. The soft pelts of rain felt good and right as she joined him in laughter.

"Wait!" He dug into his jeans pocket and plucked out his cell phone. "I sure hope this really is waterproof." He tapped once and then hit the icon. "Smile."

"You're serious?" But she did follow along—seeing them in the screen as he took selfie after selfie—and then turned her head to look into his eyes. He was so close—his face, his smile, his lips.

"Perfect, angel."

The familiar clicks fired away as she leaned in, kissing him again, knowing he was preserving this moment for the rest of time.

At least they'd have something to remember...

AN HOUR AND a half later, Molly came out of his bathroom, her bare feet softly padding on the wide-planked, honey-blond refurbished wooden floors, still drying her hair with the fluffy white towel.

She'd been amazed at the changes in the carriage house—most of all the incredible claw-foot tub he'd had installed adjacent to the skillfully tiled white with gray-veined marble walk-in shower, the new cabinet and fixtures, in the bathroom alone.

The small, yet highly functional kitchen reminded her of a chic new farmhouse and tugged at her so hard that she ached with longing.

In a few short weeks, he'd gutted the leftovers from yesteryear and rebuilt the entire second floor into a modern day living space.

Somehow, he'd created a vision she'd always wanted for her own home. *It's as if he read my mind.*

"You've done wonders with the place." Her voice croaked.

Freshly showered—she'd forced him to take one first after his dunk in the pond—he looked divine. If she could call a guy that. Bare foot, worn jeans, wearing a black Henley, Adam was definitely a sight to see.

He glanced up from where he sat on the long, medium-blue cozy-looking couch. He was leaning over and reading scattered papers on the wood and wrought iron, factory pull cart refurbished into a sleek coffee table.

"Insomnia."

"Is that what you call it?"

"Or a curse." But his slow grin took the bite out of his words.

However, his smile made her knees weak. Molly tugged at the medium-blue Henley he'd loaned her, along with his gray sweats. "Thanks."

"Looks much better on you." He nodded to her feet and picked up a pair of white socks at his side.

She glanced for another place to sit, but her damp clothes were spread out on the lone chair and ottoman. Her boots were upended on a mat beside his near the stairs.

Her toes were getting cold. She moved to sit, squeezing in beside him in the corner. Before she could object, he picked up her legs and drew them over his own.

"Red glossy nail polish. Hmm…"

She tried to tug them away, but he held fast. Then she felt the soft, cotton material on the bottoms of her feet. *The socks!* "Adam, quit. You know I'm ticklish there."

"Should I do the piggy rhyme?"

"No." But she did giggle at his silly antics.

With the utmost care, he dragged on one sock, tugging it up her calf and smoothing down the sweats over it and then repeating the actions with the other. He rubbed her feet. His warmth soon erased the cold, and the prickling sensation of blood returning took over. The heat of him seeped into her, liquefying her sore muscles and all the way to melting her bones. Something else stirred within Molly—a flame flickering, holding steady.

"Better?"

"Yes." Her voice stayed hushed in wonder.

It was as if the years of all the strife and hurt rolled away and it was just them again—Adam and Molly. Friends. Boyfriend and girlfriend. Nearly engaged. On the cusp of sharing a life together...

The silence wrapped around her like a warm, cozy blanket. Inside, more warmth spread. Lazily, she watched him, concentrating on the papers, shifting them—the soft crinkle whispering—and then going onto the next one.

Her curiosity got the better of her. "Work?"

"Catching up on the other jobs that are winding down."

Reluctantly, Molly dragged her feet back and away from his foot massage and then rested them on the floor as she sat up. She leaned against his upper arm—strong, solid, and stroking another flare of awareness in her belly—looking at the invoices.

She bit down on a sweeping wave of longing for him. "Pretty impressive, Larson." Molly didn't just mean the paperwork, either. How could he have gotten even better with time?

"My mom's handiwork here. She does my bookkeeping for the company. Went back to school for it."

"That's great. Your dad?" The last she'd heard was they'd moved to Florida soon after the wedding was called off. She often wondered about them, well, more so their only child. Adam had never been far from her thoughts.

"Went full-time as a carpenter. He creates masterpieces." Pride beamed in his voice. "In fact, I'm thinking of having him do something special for the old barn. What do you think?"

"It's perfect." She glanced at him. Big mistake. Her insides did a little tight somersault again. He was gazing at her. "Anything in mind?"

A mischievous grin tugged at his lips. "Oh, I don't know. Maybe the antler chandeliers or the trophies on the walls."

Thank goodness he switched to humor for the save. "You did not just reduce all our hard work to a stuffy lodge look? Ugh!"

"See. I told you I needed you..." He dropped his stare to her mouth and then cleared his throat. "I should take you home now." Adam moved some of the papers, several stuck out, and one threatened to fly away.

"Here." Molly grabbed for it before it went sailing. This page didn't appear to be an invoice. "Transcripts?" She blinked as she shook her head, the words not making sense. "Adam, you went to college?" Why hadn't he told her?

"It's an online thing now. They needed a copy of this.

For the prerequisites." He snatched it up and buried the paper under the pile. "Business degree. No biggie. I should at least know if I'm running my company the right way or not." The strain in his voice reverberated.

The friction radiating from him pulled her in. "Juggling business—a thriving one, at that—and school? That's amazing. By the looks of it, you aced more classes than I ever did. College, not my strong suit." She made light of it; however, it had been a long, arduous struggle to dig her mind back to something other than how attracted she still was to Adam. Not that her body followed along; it still hummed with awareness. "I'm proud of you, Adam." She meant it, for everything he'd done to better himself.

He blew out a breath and the tension siphoned out of him. "About getting you home."

"I have my SUV." She jumped up, skirted the table, and then went for her things. "Still damp." She dreaded dragging on dirty clothes after cleaning up.

"Wear mine. And I'm not letting you drive in the dark down wet, winding roads. You can pick yours up tomorrow."

Molly turned to Adam, wanting to say no. But deep inside the warmth spread. She couldn't deny how much she missed him in her life. The silly times, the caring displays—only he didn't realize he did them—and the oh, so tender moments.

Careful. You're still in hopeless romantic recovery mode, remember?

Chapter Fifteen

WITH THE RADIO volume low, the crunch of his truck's tires on the gravel driveway reverberated in the cab.

Molly shielded her eyes as the spotlight came on over the garage. She hadn't come home this late since the last time Adam had dropped her off. "Sean must have changed the light."

"I had it taken care of."

She jerked her head to see Adam shrug. His discomfort grew.

It dawned on her. "*You* did it, didn't you?"

"Nothing to it. Why bother someone else when I could do it?"

Again, the things he hadn't said spoke volumes. He'd done it for her.

There were too many questions running around in her mind as she allowed him to get her door for her and walk her to her stairs on the outside of the garage.

"Thanks. I got it from here." The cold rain pelted her cheek when she turned to him.

"Nope. It's slippery." He nudged her ahead of him.

"Hop to it."

"Drill sergeant!" She teased him now just as she had ages ago whenever that stubborn streak came through.

"Don't you know it. Come on, angel, we're both getting soaked."

Why did she have to like this part of him? The concerned, caring guy who called her angel. *Yeah, that one really tugs at my heart.*

She clomped up the wooden stairs in her heavy boots and he did right behind her, shielding her from the back and side. At the top, Molly fumbled in the small compartment in her camera bag. The jangle of keys masked the sudden whip of wind.

Getting the door unlocked, she shoved it open, rushed in dragging Adam behind her, wiped her boots on the mat, and then flicked on the overhead light. "The storm is kicking up. You can wait out the worst here." It was the least she could do.

He shut the door with a definite click, ran a hand down his wet face, and then through his hair. Adam gazed around her small apartment, if one could even call it that.

"I'll get you a towel." She toed off her boots and padded to the bathroom, still wearing his white socks. She grabbed two fluffy pink ones and brought them back.

Adam stood in the exact same spot as she left him, alert, taking in her tiny abode with the flea market finds and repurposed furniture. He did accept her offering and began to wipe down.

"Nice place."

"It's the best I could convince my parents to do—discounted white paint, new beige carpet at the time, updated plumbing and electric. I think they did the minimal, hoping I'd fly the not-so-nice nest sooner rather than later and find a new man instead of me getting too comfortable here." She gulped at the things she'd revealed to him. *Stop, already.*

"Dark room still in the back of the garage?"

"Of course. My one perk." He remembered her obsession of staying in there for hours developing photos instead of waiting for the one at school to reopen during sane hours.

Quiet settled around them, making her highly aware of being alone with him again. She shivered from his heated look.

"Come on in. I can make some coffee, well, I think there's a bit left over." She shot him a self-deprecating grin. "I'm off the caffeinated stuff. Makes me all jittery and nervous. Not unlike how I'm feeling around you right now."

She stilled.

He did, too.

"Did I really just say that out loud?" She groaned, clearly having let the words trip out.

There was a sudden pounding on her door, making them both jump and turn to it.

"Molly! Who do you have in there with you?" Her mother's familiar voice rang out.

"Mom? You're here?" Her heart didn't simmer down at all on that realization.

"Open the door!" Her father nearly bellowed. "There's a

strange truck in the driveway."

"They're really back?" Her mind reeled.

Slack-jawed, she jerked to look at Adam. Guilt and anxiety bubbled up inside her. His features went stone cold, like granite.

"Shall I?" Before she could answer, Adam reached out, twisted the knob, and then opened the door. "Mr. and Mrs. McCleary, what a surprise."

"Adam," Molly hissed under her breath. Shock took over her beloved parents' faces—a little pasty under their tans.

Molly infused cheer into herself where dread threatened to take over. "Hey, Mom, Dad. You're back early. Days early." *Why now? Why ruin my happy time? Wow, where had that come from?*

"Y-you?" Her mother marched in—looking well-rested, her blondish, wavy hair with the faint streaks of gray tumbling to her shoulders now, and none the worse for wear from her nearly one-year sabbatical—glaring at Adam, and dragging Molly's dad by the sleeve. Her dad—tall with dark hair—dropped the soaked, navy blue umbrella near the shoe stand.

"No need for introductions, are there?" Molly's teeth chattered. She hugged herself, still clutching the pink towel.

"Whose clothes are those? His?"

"Mom, I missed you, too." Well, a little. But not at the moment. Molly sensed the standoff between Adam and her parents.

"Not now, Molly. Really, you have a terrible sense of timing."

"I could say the same for you, too, Mom." The words popped out.

A ball of tangled heat sat in Molly's chest. A niggling memory returned of her folks and Adam sizing each other up when they were all together for some family thing or sporting event. She'd shoved the tension down then, brushing it away, and assumed it would eventually dissipate after their wedding. Now, not so much.

"Welcome back to Cupid's Corner." Adam broke the awkward stretch of silence. He turned to Molly and handed over his towel. "I'll be going now, angel." Leaning down, he kissed her soft and tender on her cheek.

Both her parents gasped at his audacity.

However, it made Molly all warm and fuzzy again. She caught and held his stare. His green eyes were filled with hurt. Molly ached for him. How could she let him know she didn't agree with them or their harsh, snap condemnations?

Reaching out, she touched his wrist, dropping it to his fisted left hand, waiting until he relaxed his fingers, uncurling them.

He let out an unsteady breath. "Thanks."

A few moments later, she closed the door behind him, waited to hear his footsteps pound down the wooden stairs, and then faintly cross the gravel. Molly turned to her folks, who slumped into her dining room chairs, and then she rushed to the large front window. She smoothed back the curtains to watch him.

Adam must have seen her; the lights went off and came back on twice—their special good-night signal.

Molly smiled sadly at the hollow ache sweeping over her as he reversed his truck out of the driveway, turned it, and then left.

"How could you do this to us?" her mother asked.

Swallowing the lump lodged in her throat, Molly turned to her mom and dad. "Can I at least get a hug from you two first?"

A HALF HOUR later, Molly really wished she had the last dregs of coffee in the pot. But no, she held on to her silly caffeinated recovery mode. Why? She had no clue.

"It's just shocking. To come home after nearly a year away and find *him* in our home."

"*My* apartment." Molly didn't miss the covert looks between her parents.

"You don't pay rent, dear." Her father's accounting background kicked in. "We *allow* you to live here." He sipped from his mug.

That could have been my java. Maybe I need to rethink my foolish ways. "Point taken, Daddy." But something grated along Molly's nerves.

"The places we've seen and stayed at these last months. Why, nowadays, we could get a pretty penny for something like this, couldn't we, dear?" He gazed around, nodding his head. "You can move back in the house with us."

Another belly clench had Molly gripping her glass of cool water. This was not going well at all. They'd never questioned it or even brought it up in nearly six years. Why now? "Does this have anything to do with my seeing Adam again?" *Oops! Those words really should not have been spoken.*

Her mother pressed a hand to her chest. "You…are not… No, never again. He dumped you, may I remind you, Molly?"

"Ouch!" *I really need to put a lid on this wayward mouth of mine. At least, it seems, they haven't heard about the fake reunion stuff.* Silently, she thanked her brother for not spilling the beans and clueing them into the Cupid's Corner gossip.

Her dad leaned his forearms on the table. "Yes, it does. He's not to come around here. He's done enough damage all those years ago."

"Don't you think I should be the judge of that?" Molly shook her head, wondering when she'd gotten so bold as to question her devoted parents. "I'm different now."

"Oh, please. That good-looking boy just comes and goes, drops you, and then comes back and expects to pick things up where you left off? And you're falling for it. Dear, we know best. He's not the one for you." Her mother's arch of her eyebrows added to the overall effect.

Molly let it sink in—the present stance mixing with the past warnings—and didn't appreciate the overprotective nature one bit.

They grew anxious when she cried, laughed too loud, played too hard, or squealed with excitement. All as if they couldn't cope with her range of feelings and needed to contain them—neutralize the hiccup to the smooth, sedate, protective life they'd created for her. So, she'd conformed to their tense reprimands—verbal and otherwise.

She'd ignored it then, going along as she'd always done from childhood—keeping the peace and not upsetting the cart or anyone except herself.

Until Adam…

However, all the telltale signs were there—Adam didn't fit their vision of who she should marry. He was big and bold and fascinating to her, then and now. There'd been no way to hide the way she lit up whenever he was mentioned or around her.

The warnings were subtle then, brushing off Adam and her silly youthful dreams. No, *crush*, that was what they'd said.

"I've grown up." Who was she trying to convince? But she sat up straighter. "You haven't seen it or me this last year. I own my own photography business—"

"Thanks to your brother for giving you the deposit." Her dad smirked. "Against our better wishes. You had a perfectly good job with the school taking pictures. Steady income, benefits, even a small retirement plan. You threw it all away."

Her throat squeezed. "I still do the school photos, only I set the time and price. I don't answer to anyone." *I love taking funny pictures of the triplets and now even more kids, thanks to the word of mouth around town. And I'd never give up this chance to create the wedding venue or work alongside Adam.*

"Maybe that's the problem. You don't live in the real world."

If anything could've shaken her more than that Molly couldn't have ever possibly guessed what would.

They saw her as weak and needy. Still.

She'd been sheltered and coddled her entire life, wrapped up in wool to never bruise or to shatter her fragile nature.

The truth hit hard.

Was she clinging to Adam again to feel safe and protected and avoid standing on her own two feet?

Chapter Sixteen

ADAM CLENCHED THE steering wheel with both hands on the short, but winding ride back to the carriage house. His knuckles ached, but he didn't let up.

His past reared up and punched him in the gut, quick and sharp.

The McClearys hadn't been as vocal while Molly and he were in high school. The body language and stern looks had revealed much more.

He cringed at the first meeting of their parents at the sophomore homecoming football game. Stiff, awkward, and glaringly obvious they were from two different worlds—professional and working class—attempting to unite. But there were more hints and signs…

Not good enough for their Molly. Not some guy from the wrong side of the tracks.

"Let's not upset Molly." Her mother had often cautioned her husband when he'd tried to talk sense into them whenever the subject of them getting married after graduation came up. "No need to bring that up now. We'll deal with it later."

A sick sinking sensation flooded Adam. Pieces began to

fall into place.

His senior English teacher had marked up his final seven-page essay in red pen—so much so, it looked like a kid had scribbled all over it. She'd given him his first *D* ever, the score making up over half of his grade that year, dragging it down. Reluctantly, she'd refused his year-long, extra credit book reports, citing the class advisor—Mrs. McCleary—ruled against the favoritism it implied. And Adam had tried so hard to maintain his GPA for…

"College." His stunned word echoed through the truck cab as he turned into the driveway. *The scholarship. Gone.*

In the rain, he noticed old man Pickens waving him down near the back of the old Victorian house.

Adam's aching chest couldn't take any more bad news.

He powered down the window as he drew alongside and halted. The misty rain came in and Adam blinked away the moisture. "You all right?"

"Me? Sure. I saw some lights in the barn about twenty minutes ago and came out to check. I chased off some kids. Curious, I guess. That makes the second bunch this week and about five overall now."

"Daring each other?" Adam remembered those times well. "No harm, right?"

"Nah. Just keeping me on my toes. Speaking of which, my boots are soaked through."

"Got any coffee?" Adam tipped his head to the entrance near the old kitchen. He needed to stay away from the carriage house for a while and the deep longing for Molly to be there when he got in. She belonged there. It felt so right and so very perfect for her to be there earlier.

"Sure do. Always got a pot going from five a.m. to ten p.m. Come on, son."

Adam shot him a tight smile before putting the window back up, driving the last few yards to the carriage house and parking it there, and then getting out and sprinting through the rain to the house. His boots made smacking noises in the puddles.

He knocked twice before he opened the door, greeted by the worn room and the delicious scent of strong coffee. The old black woodstove in the corner put out some welcoming heat. Pickens's wet boots were already beside it.

"Got us a treat tonight." Pickens popped open the metal cover of the shortbread cookie tin. "Good for dipping."

Settling in at the large, oblong wood table with the faded blue-and-white-checkered plastic tablecloth, Adam gladly accepted the white mug, took a quick sip, and then grabbed a couple of buttery yellow cookies. "Good."

"What's on your mind?" The man grunted and groaned as he took a chair beside Adam.

"That bad?" Yeah, if his face revealed every churning emotion inside, it looked terrible.

"A little gray around the gills."

He tried to brush aside his lingering dread. "If the skies clear up tomorrow, we can get back to some real work."

"You can't fool me." Pickens looked over the rim of his chipped mustache mug and then took a swig. "What's really bothering you? That sweet girl of yours?"

Deny. Deny. Deny. Adam shrugged. He dipped one of his

cookies in his coffee and took a soggy bite, chewing it instead of answering.

"Fact is… She's real quiet, staying in the background so much a soul doesn't even know she's there most times, taking picture after picture, hiding behind her camera—'cause you see a whole lot more by observing and listening than by talking. She's been that way for years, except when she's with you. Yep, saw it back in the day with you two. Now, even more. Don't think I've seen it? Ha! Both of you brighten up like lightning bugs in a jar, making everything around you come to life, too."

Adam swallowed the treat and hastily drank some more bitter coffee. Looking back, everything the older man said was spot-on. Molly and Adam were high school sweethearts in love. Of course it showed. Now though? He adored her so much he ached with it. But he'd hurt her.

Just seeing her parents' reaction to him tonight dredged up a lot of old baggage. He wasn't good enough for their daughter. Then. Still.

In their eyes, he'd remained the boy who would never be on the same level as their daughter.

He would have to work hard to cover up his feelings in front of them from now on to protect Molly from any backlash. However, he couldn't resist a little jab at his friend. "Practicing poetic speeches for the weddings, Pick?"

"Hiring me on?" He rubbed his hands together. "I can sprout off until the cows come home."

Laughing, Adam noted how it shifted all his broken pieces inside as shafts of pain sliced through him. "Always could tell a good story."

"That I can."

"Ever think about getting one of those online justice of the peace certificates? You could actually be the one to marry couples." The image brought a slight smile to Adam.

"Me? Never thought about it…" He nodded. "So, getting back to business. About the girl, Molly."

Blowing out a pent-up breath from his lungs, Adam shook his head. "Missed my chance."

"Fool me once, shame on you. Fool me twice, shame on me."

Frowning, Adam looked up. "What?"

"Yep, I figured you were just marking time with her back then. Different, but in a good way. Then just like that"—he snapped his fingers—"you dump her—"

"It was as awful as you make it sound. The breaking up. The rest was real." Could he just stop these waves of pain crashing over him?

"That's what was puzzling to me. You were smitten with her and then bang gone. You didn't even show up for your own graduation."

Adam gritted his teeth, recalling the utter failure pulsing through him at missing out on his college scholarship.

"'Course everyone heaped the blame on you."

"Rightly so." His chest squeezed.

Pickens slapped his hands on the tabletop, causing the unfastened cookie tin lid to jump and jangle. "Then you call me out of the blue, buy the place, and then show up on my doorstep. You didn't stay away. So that got me to thinking."

"You know, you do too much of that and it will give you migraines." Adam tried to keep it light as the older man circled around him.

The man rubbed his thumb and finger over his bearded chin. "One of three things. You want to make amends. You want to prove you made it. Or you want to make sure you did the right thing by walking away and giving Molly a decent chance in life."

If he'd taken a sledgehammer and whacked him in the gut with it, it wouldn't have hurt as much as the older man's words did—because, dang, if the truth didn't leave a mark.

Molly, I didn't want to ruin your life then. Now, either. But I can't stay away from you. Maybe I can do something more to beg for your forgiveness once and for all so I can live with myself again...

"FIFTY *PITY* PERCENT?" Molly scowled at Adam over the counter in her studio. *Seriously? Guilt, that had to be it after seeing her parents and their reactions.*

He'd picked her up early, brought her here, and then stayed. His unusual quietness settled like a hushed expectancy.

The pitter-patter of rain outside made it intimate and unnerving at the same time.

Something had been brewing obviously through her two portrait sittings—a sweet older couple's fifty-fifth anniversary photo and a redo for a senior picture, the tall, lanky kid wanted to wear his racing gear and holding his black and green helmet instead of the traditional boring mortarboard one.

They were gone. Her appointments done. Yet Adam remained, at times sending text messages or glued to his computer he'd set up right beside hers.

Now, Adam gripped his hands on the edge of the counter. "You say that as if it's a bad thing."

She laughed. "Oh, what am I going to do with you? Look, I'm good." But she stopped, swallowing hard. After the confrontation with her parents last night, she wondered where she stood with anything. "Well, I will be soon."

"I need a wedding coordinator."

He dropped the offer into the air and Molly jerked back. "Wh-what?" Her heart galloped.

"On-site. Wedding and events."

"You're serious?"

"My business is over an hour away. My executive assistant, Mrs. Sanderson—you've talked to her a couple of times for orders—is doing this remotely. Yeah, not working out. She's inundated with calls for bookings, questions, you name it."

Molly's legs shook. She backed up, using her hand to find the stool, and then sank down on it.

Adam came around the counter and plopped down in a facing stool, using his feet to roll it closer to her. "With what's planned already, this summer it earns out, paying me back for the reno. I keep the land and buildings. We split the wedding and event venue profits after that."

She dragged in a heavy breath and then another. "You're teasing me, Larson."

"No joke, Moll. You get full rein of the property for your photography…even relocate this place up there on the hill, if you want. Can you imagine all the great shots? Natural lighting?"

"I could do so much more." Her mind whirled with the possibilities and the wide open spaces. Ideas and hopes sparked to life. "I'm dreaming, right?"

He smiled then, his green eyes lit from within. "It's yours. Take it."

Deep inside, she yearned to say yes. But something held her back. Her thoughts went to the repercussions. "There'd be talk. About us." Especially when he walked away again.

"Like that hasn't happened before." He grimaced.

"M-my mom and dad." The words hung between them, cracking open the place neither one of them really wanted to go.

Adam searched her face and then held her gaze. "Was it that bad after I left?"

She lifted her hand and tilted it back and forth. On the outside, she tried to keep her features calm. However, her insides clenched.

"Let me guess. They don't like me being anywhere near you."

"Wow, good guess." She tried to force her lips into a smile, but the bottom one trembled a little.

His stare landed there. "They'll never forgive me for what I did to you. It's their burden, not mine. I can't go back. I can't change them. I don't even want to do that for me. *You*, yes. I've always wanted more for you. I went about it all wrong the first time. But this time, right now, has always been about us. Will you forgive me, Moll? Someday?" His question came out raw and scratchy.

Chapter Seventeen

MOLLY FOCUSED ON the computer screen, highly aware of Adam beside her working on his laptop—updating his business website with her photos of the property and them—as the morning rain slowly began to lift outside. She'd already uploaded a few of them at her own website, carefully guarding anything telling.

If he shifted just so, he'd brush his shoulder against hers every now and then, sending sparks and tingles through her veins.

The man was incredibly sexy and dangerous.

Her email dinged. She clicked on it and opened the latest one.

Please.

Quit. She sent Adam a response.

Pretty please?

She giggled, turning to catch a glimpse of his grinning profile. She peeked at what he was doing now. Part of the page revealed what looked like his college class notes. The other was his open email.

Turning back to the task at hand, Molly cropped the image—too much background for her taste—and flicked through the next two. She'd present them to her new client from the other day, pictures of the young mother's three-year-old son with the biggest smile on his face as he sat behind the wheel in his favorite green kid's mini-truck.

Molly's heart hitched. She'd longed for a little boy with Adam—the same soft, light brown hair that had gentle waves in it when it was long and the same melting green eyes. *Did my insides just quiver or quake? Yeah, one of those.*

The ding came again. Molly blinked away the threatening moisture in the corners of her eyes and absently clicked open Adam's email, thinking it was another plea for her to agree to his partnership.

She gasped at the image. "Th-that's us! From the boat." Molly leaned in, drinking in every aspect from their heads touching, to their smiles and glowing faces, to the spark in their eyes. Then she clicked on the other one—where they'd kissed, getting drenched, but not caring.

Toggling back and forth, Molly read the unspoken truth she was too afraid to confront before. *Adam! You never stopped loving me.*

It took all her effort not to look at herself—vulnerable and exposed to the lens. Something she'd avoided for most of her life.

Hiding behind it was so much easier.

The jangle of the door opening behind her caused Molly to suck in a startled breath, jump up, and will the guilty heat from her cheeks away as she faced her next customer. Her mouth dropped open. "Bernard?" What was he doing here?

And his newspaper reporter nose took in every little dang thing.

"My, what do we have here? Cupid's Corner lovebirds." His voice boomed, cutting through the comfortable silence. "Cozy?"

Adam twirled around on the stool. "If it isn't Bernie." He stood, extending a hand. He nodded to the open pad and pencil in the older man's hand. "Still at it, I see."

"Looks like you two are, too. I had to come and get the scoop in person." He lifted his cell phone and snapped off a few shots.

Molly blinked. "What was that for?"

"*Cupid's Corner Gazette*, of course. You're doing the pictures for the paper and I'm doing the article. I think we'll do a series on the couple behind the renovation."

"Couple?" Her voice squeaked. This fake reunion was getting dicey, nonexistent as it was. What would her parents have to say about the growing gossip? *Yikes.*

"Great human interest angle, don't you think? High school sweethearts reuniting for a second chance. How's that?"

"Not good," Molly whispered under her breath.

She glanced over at Adam and he stared at her with a perplexed frown.

"Don't look at me. I agreed to an interview. Nothing more." Adam seemed genuine.

"This isn't about the, uh, business arrangement?" Molly nudged his toe with her boot.

"What's that, you say?" Bernard held his hand up to the

back of his ear.

"Just ideas." She brushed it away.

"Actually, Bernie, we're going in as full partners—" Adam halted when she stomped on his foot. "Whoa! Did you just—" He pasted on a fake grin. "She's shy." However, he did move away, putting distance between them. "With a mean temper. Who knew?"

"Adam, you can stop talking anytime…"

He hobbled around the counter and snagged Bernard by the arm, directing him away and toward the door. "Maybe now isn't the best time. Tomorrow morning at nine at the barn? We, uh, I can show you around. Is that good for you?"

"Works for me." Bernard tapped his pencil on the pad. "In the meantime, I'll dig into the history of the place more. Fascinating stuff. And search the archives for your high school pictures. Before and after. Then and now." Bernard glanced back. "Molly, don't forget to send those kids' engagement photo to go with the announcement. It's coming out in Sunday's edition."

"Will do." Molly gulped hard. Kyle and Kyra's photos were perfect and they'd selected one to go in the paper. Something about all things weddings jammed her up inside.

"Yours and Adam's current pictures, too. We'll do a special feature on you two, maybe spread it over a few issues. Love is in the air, by golly!"

How was she going to survive the next few weeks leading up to all of the happy nuptials, especially now as Adam came back and faced her with a chagrined look on his face?

Her heart tugged so hard she was certain it was going to

leap out of her chest at any moment.

No, she couldn't go through this again. Waiting, wondering, being tangled up in knots, and then the excruciating pain that followed.

There were no do-overs for her. Nor were there second chances anywhere in her future…

ADAM STOOD BACK as Molly locked the door of her shop, flicking the key with some definite muscle behind it to make the lock click loudly.

She'd been unusually quiet after Bernard's exit a half hour ago. More so after Adam sent the picture of them in the boat—the smiling one—as their recent photo.

It was utterly perfect. His picture-perfect bride—only she wasn't a bride or his anymore. That last part stung.

He'd added a few lines and the date of the opening event. Just weeks away.

"Don't you want to talk about it?"

"Which part?" She turned to him, rolling her eyes. "How do I let these things happen to me? You tell me."

"What, uh, things exactly?" He shouldn't ask if he didn't want to hear the answer.

"Everyone, including you, Adam Larson, pushes and pulls me in directions I don't want to go in." She marched down the street, sidestepping puddles, as the sun slowly burned away the last of the raindrops.

"You're mad." He could kick himself right about now.

She'd lumped him in with the others—her family, even. Molly looked over her shoulder. "Heck, yes, I am."

"Seething? Or simmering?" He strolled beside her down the cobblestoned sidewalk and hopefully toward his truck in the town square. She still had her SUV at the barn.

"Almost to a boil, how's that?" She stomped through a puddle, splashing water on her jeans and his, and continued on.

"Interesting." He tried to add some humor to it, following in her wake.

"Just interesting?"

"Well, I can't remember you ever being mildly upset, come to think of it."

"Oh, believe me, I was. I just never showed it."

"At me?"

She mulled it over. "Besides the dumping part? Let's see…"

"Sorry I asked." But he grinned. He liked this Molly—real, raw, and fascinating.

Molly halted at the corner of Main and Vine, facing him. "You irritated me a time or a half dozen, but nothing major. Mostly, it was about you not—"

He stilled. "What?"

"Not seeing yourself as I did." Her soft voice wrapped around him.

She hit too close to home. *Yep, right there in the solar plexus.*

Adam shrugged. "So, we're good then?" He strode away, half hoping she wouldn't follow.

Of course, she did. Her footsteps got louder as he picked up his pace. "We're not done talking."

Groaning, Adam reached his truck and opened her door. "Now? You decide you want to talk now?"

Molly hopped in. "Why not? You asked for it. I'll have you in a confined space for nearly twenty minutes."

"Hostage takeover?" Adam dragged his feet to his side, took his sweet time hauling himself in, and then started it up. "Okay, go for it."

She didn't utter a word.

He glanced over at her as he halted at the exit to turn onto the road. Her pale face and wide, striking blue eyes nailed him in the gut. "Moll?"

Clearing her throat, she turned to look out the windshield and grip the door handle. "I think it's the first time you or anyone really asked me to talk—about serious stuff."

A ripple of regret shot through him. "Was I that bad?"

"Just hyperfocused on getting good grades, winning football games, and...digging your way out of your circumstances." She swallowed hard. "Drive. Determination. I didn't understand then. I think I do now."

He powered down his window, sucking in fresh, clean rain-scented air as he drove out of town.

"You're trying to help me do that, too, aren't you?"

Shock raced down his spine. A couple of months ago, he'd seen her byline in the online edition of the *Cupid's Corner Gazette* of the picture of her brother, Sean, and Gemma kissing on Valentine's Day.

Somehow, he could see Molly behind the scenes, documenting other people's happiness while sitting on the sidelines. Deep inside, he knew he'd done that to her—made her cautious and weary and hesitant to jump into life when all he'd ever wanted to do was give her one, even if that meant without him.

"Guilty." He fessed up to his role.

"It's not that awful, you know."

"You deserve more. More than I could have given you back then."

"When did you get to decide for me? Why does everyone feel like they know better than I do?"

Adam watched the two-lane street, not daring to look over at her. He continued on for miles, turning at the right roads, and then up the hill. "Truth?"

"You owe me that at least, Adam."

It hurt down to his bones. He waited until he pulled into the driveway to the barn, the tires slowly crunching on the gravel. After he parked and shut off the engine, he turned to her. Sunlight peeked out of the clouds overhead and dabbled through the tree branches.

Her gorgeous blue eyes pinned him to the spot.

She was beautiful and amazing and he had to tell her. He sucked in a tight breath. "You let them, Moll."

That little frown on her brow came. "Me?"

"Yeah." The band around his chest squeezed. "Whatever they fed you—fragile, helpless, needy, unsure, weak, even if it were a smidgen true at one brief time when you were born a preemie—you believed that about yourself. Forever." The things he said to her were hitting him hard and fast, too. He believed the garbage other people thought about him.

Only Molly never treated him like that.

He'd hurt the one incredible, amazing woman who had championed him…

Chapter Eighteen

MOLLY GAWKED AT Adam, reading the pain and sincerity in his eyes. Like a mirror, she saw herself, recalling the many, many times she stayed tight-lipped, even when she was shouting on the inside. How many fights had she avoided by not speaking up or out? She'd been a pushover.

No conflict allowed.

The day Adam had left, she could have rallied or screamed or even begged. All she'd done was cry, feel his warm, strong arms around her one last time, press into him for the soft kiss on her forehead, and then watch him walk away.

And her heart crumbled into tiny little pieces. Shattered.

Without one word on how I felt. On what I wanted. I would have gone to the ends of the earth with you, Adam. But I never had the guts to tell you that.

She gasped. "I *do* do that…go along, let people make decisions for me, not make waves or upset people…" She clenched her eyes closed, trying to ward off more agonizing scenes flashing before her. "It's easier. No real decisions. No real blame."

He reached out for her hand.

Molly curled her fingers into her palms. "I'm so angry with myself right now. I—I need time."

"As long as you want." He tilted his head toward the empty yard, littered with construction material covered in tarp, and then the barn. "Crew is off for the rest of the day. The rain drenched most everything." His rough voice rumbled through the cab.

She shivered in spite of herself. Warding off the heady attraction to Adam took a will of steel, something she obviously lacked in all areas of her life to date.

"I've got an extra hammer if you want to blow off some steam."

Me? I never do those kinds of things. Not the physical stuff. "Why not?" It was the first real spontaneous decision she'd ever made.

Hopefully, she wouldn't regret it.

TWO HOURS LATER, Molly's shoulders burned and her arms quivered. Still, she swung the heavy sledgehammer, aiming and cracking the old lumber in what Adam described as the bridal waiting area. Only it was a decent, oversized shed moved from another part of the farm two days ago and set down on now level ground on the other side of the barn, like a smaller, cuter counterpoint to the carriage house to the right.

Opening the space took muscle, which she had little of. Adam worked alongside her, kicking down boards, yanking out spikes or rusty nails, and flinging his regular hammer.

The man had moves. *Just saying.*

Her anger boiled over after the first couple of swipes. Then she'd put her weight behind it and really went to work, releasing the pent-up, churning emotions with grunts, yells, and then guttural cries. Tears came, dried in streaks, and then evaporated.

Adam didn't run or hide.

Amazing man. *Observing, all right?*

"Onc more." She gritted her teeth over a very stubborn section.

Molly raised the sledgehammer over her head and swung with all the might she had left in her. The wood splintered, but didn't budge. She dropped the heavy piece to the floor—it landed with a thud—and gasped for breath. She took off one work glove to swipe the rivulets of sweat off her forehead with the back of her hand.

"Don't be a weenie."

Molly jerked her head up and faced a grinning Adam, who leaned against a wall, with his white hardhat tilted back. Dirt covered part of his handsome face, making his white teeth stand out. Delight and a challenge danced in his eyes.

"Give up now and it beat you, Moll."

This wasn't just about an ancient wall. This was about her and the power she wielded.

She yanked her glove back on and set her pink hardhat in place. "Five bucks says I can take that down in two more swings."

"Five? Come on. You can do better than that."

"Name it." Two can play at this game.

"Fancy-schmancy dinner out. Dress to the nines?" He shrugged. "You and me, Moll, just like we said we'd do when we made it big."

Her breath stayed trapped in her lungs. He remembered their long ago vow.

He dug in his jeans pocket, pulled out a key, and then dangled it. "Carriage house apartment, too. You can live in it after I move out, say for the next year. Pay me the going rate of rent, if you insist."

Something light and beautiful grew inside her, pushing out the darkness she'd felt these last hours. She loved the space he'd redone—everything about it. Work here and live here, doing it her way? He offered Molly the precious gift of her independence. "Get ready to pay up, Larson."

"Those are definitely fighting words. Show me what you got, McCleary."

Instead of taking a shot, Molly eyed the structure, noted the crack, and then walked around it, sizing it up where she'd put a dent in it. She came back to her original spot.

She nodded to her camera in the corner. "You need to get this on film to preserve it for the rest of time, buddy."

Adam threw back his head and laughed. It was rich and real and the sweetest sound she'd ever heard.

He came back with it, aiming it.

"Ready?"

"Go!"

First, she looked straight at the lens, knowing he watched her intently. Then she winked.

"Sassy."

"Yep! Watch me now!" Molly sucked in a breath against the pain, raised the heavy sledgehammer, took a step forward, and then smashed it into the wall, leaving a big, gaping hole. She stepped back and then repeated the motion right beside the first one, this time breaking through—wood cracked and splintered—the wall creaked and toppled over.

Stunned wonder rippled through her.

"You did it, Moll!"

"Adam, I did it!" She rushed to him.

"Whoa, hammer."

She dropped it and it landed with a heavy *thunk*. Molly stepped forward, hugging him close. The clicks in her ear made her chuckle. "You can stop filming now, Adam, and hug me back."

He did. "Yes, ma'am." However, he picked her up with one arm and swung her around. "And the champion of all time is Molly McCleary!"

Molly threw back her head and soaked up the moment of triumph in Adam's warm, strong arms.

DAYS FLEW INTO weeks and Molly found an inner strength she never knew she had.

The triple life of photographer, reno helper, and event coordinator was exhausting and exhilarating at the same time.

There was a spark lit inside her that hadn't been there before. It radiated through her and out of her.

Along with her ever present camera, she carried a planner of all things. Her? The one who used scraps of papers and sticky notes to remember things? The sleek new pink planner filled up with numerous meetings with contractors, caterers, florists, events, brides and grooms, and her own studio appointments saved her on numerous occasions.

And there was gorgeous Adam—attentive, focused, thriving, and still out of reach.

She kept it that way.

Friends? How could she downsize their relationship to a minuscule part of her life? But she had for her sanity.

Asking for time had put up a no-cross barrier, yet it freed them both to be more of themselves than ever before.

In spite of the growing curiosity from his crew, friends, family—yeah, not going there with her parents' many heated discussions—and townspeople, along with the never-ending questions from Bernard for the *Gazette* articles, Adam and Molly remained polite yet distant in their united front.

Molly ached for Adam, even when he was just a few feet away. And the way he gazed longingly back at her... *Yeah, no one's kidding anyone here.*

But they made it work so far.

One fake couple playing at planning a pretend wedding. Correction, opening event of a pseudo wedding to market to the industry.

Everything went smoothly. That was why she hated to

initiate this part today. She politely knocked on the beautifully sanded and newly stained wooden carriage house door a few times and instantly got an answer, her hand poised in midair for another one.

"Oh." She pulled away and held her camera—her barrier.

By silent agreement, they'd stayed away from personal space, like his place and hers.

"Hey, did I miss something?" Adam blinked, frowning at her.

She gulped. It had been difficult to avoid staring at him for days upon days, but now she had no choice. *Like I need an excuse to gawk.*

Adam's tall frame filled the doorway. She felt his body heat from where she stood. *Very warm and alluring.* His well-worn jeans hugged him. The black T-shirt he wore molded to his wide chest and she could barely drag her gaze away from the tight material, or rather what lay beneath.

However, she forced herself to lift her hungry gaze to his handsome face and dreamy eyes. Her knees wobbled. Her thoughts scrambled.

"Uh, if we want those shots, you know, for the brochure, it's a no-go for Kyra and Kyle. They're both sick." She drew in a shaky breath. "So, it's you and me."

"This is a joke, right?" His growing smile knocked the wind out of her lungs.

Molly stuck her thumb over her shoulder. "I brought the dress-up costumes from my stash at my shop. Unless you have a better idea." Hope filled her words. Pretending meant pushing the blurry lines even more.

"I'm game. Are you?"

She was afraid he'd say that…

Hours flew by as Molly and Adam debated—mildly and silly opposing views—on the right spots on the property, somewhat coordinated dress wear, and several poses.

He'd gone for the close-ups, while she preferred the long shots that highlighted the area—farm, pond, newly redone parts of the barn, and even Mr. Pickens's refurbished old red pickup truck parked near the entrance where sweet-smelling wildflowers grew.

She laughed at Adam's antics, caught up in his ability to let down his guard on film. She'd never felt comfortable doing that before, keeping herself firmly behind the camera and in her subdued place. But with Adam, chasing him and then running beside him in the nearby field, she was lighter, happier.

Molly had even let him take a few shots of her alone—in several outfit changes from a long, silk lavender gown to more casual jean shorts and a feminine floral top and then to his preferred one of her in a blue thigh-length dress with sheer long sleeves and overlay and a slightly flared skirt.

Her shyness melted away by slow degrees with each click. Or was it because it was Adam looking at her through the lens?

"Great one! Yeah, when you twirled like that." Adam stood stock-still, holding the camera away from his eye. "The sun catches your red hair…"

"Take the picture already, Adam." She smiled, soft

springy green grass beneath her bare feet, and went around in another circle. A few yellow butterflies fluttered up and around. She laughed.

"Got it!"

But she didn't stop. She held out her arms, breathing in the fresh, late-morning air and soaking in the warmth of the sun on her upturned face. No boundaries or barriers. *Free.*

In moments, Adam joined her, moving with her as she wrapped her arms loosely around his neck, and taking his beloved zoomed-in shots. He held the camera up and away, allowing it to capture both of them in rapid succession.

"You're not doing what I think you are, are you?"

"I am." His grin widened.

"But I never show myself, not like this—"

"It's time you start, angel, to see the best of who you are. The way I see you."

Molly's breath shuttered out of her and she leaned in, capturing his warm, intent stare before she pressed her lips against his. He kissed her, so sweet and tender. *Heaven.*

Yep, lines definitely blurred. She could almost imagine this was real and it was all about them. The ache of want inside her unfurled and spread to the tips of her fingers and toes.

How am I ever going to let you go, Adam?

"OVER HERE, MOLL!" Gemma waved to her from the edge of the water ten feet away.

Coming down the last of the hill, Molly veered direction.

"What, no bench? Do you have a fever, cough, cold? You're not yourself, Gem." She grinned, giving her bestie a brief hug.

It seemed like forever since she'd seen Gemma. Molly had so much to tell her and catch up on after the last weeks of nonstop going for the venue and her growing business.

However, her friend didn't return the cheer, only a fiercer embrace. Finally, Gemma let her go.

Her eyes were clouded with concern. "Ah, she didn't tell you, did she?"

"Who's she?" Molly was the one who usually talked in code, not her practical, librarian best friend.

"Your mom."

Her belly sank. Covertly, she looked around. "She here?"

"At Cuppa Joe with your dad and Sean. Waiting on us to join them."

"But that's Sean and your special place where you meet up every few days to go over the Dear Cupid letters for the *Gazette*."

"That was sidelined. They want to discuss wedding details with us." She shook her head. "Most of it is taken care of already. You know my grams, she's been looking forward to this day since I was born. Other than stopping her idea for a parade—can you imagine Sean and me celebrating our nuptials in the middle of chaos?"

Molly smiled, knowing Mrs. V.'s exuberance when it came to all things love. Yeah, she really adored that lady. Always had. "So, it's just a going over of the plan thing?"

"Not really." She winced, looked up the hill, and then

moved Molly a few feet away and toward the pond. "Sean kind of clued me in before we got here."

Something hard and heavy dropped in Molly's gut. Dawning rushed in. She hadn't seen this coming from a mile away. Maybe because she had more important things to do with her time. "Me. It's about me." She took in little gasps of air. "And Adam."

"All things point to it, Moll."

"You're trying to warn me before we head in." But that wasn't the drill. Molly met Gemma here every time her best friend had a day off and before she joined Sean at Cuppa Joe. It worked for months now. Molly didn't infringe on them, the little time they had together right now, or be that awkward, uncomfortable third wheel.

Gemma touched her arm, turning her slightly away from the view of the pond and attempting to get Molly to look at her. "He hurt you once."

"Are you on their side?" That stung.

"No. I'm with you. All the way. I just have to be the voice of reason right now. You still care about him. I'm pretty sure he does for you, too, by the way he looks at you..."

"Yeah, he does." Molly knew that with certainty deep in her bones.

A man didn't look at a woman with such longing and tenderness without something more behind it, not when he was the perfect gentleman and only wanted the best for her, even if it meant he couldn't be in her life.

"If or when he leaves again?" Gemma left it hanging in

the air.

That thought remained a constant, unwelcome nagging concern to Molly.

She let out a shaky sigh. "I'll live." *With my heart ripped apart again if I'm not careful.*

Her best friend pulled her head back slightly. "It's too late already, isn't it?"

"Gem, I never stopped." There, she'd said it, simple words that revealed everything she'd hidden for all these years.

"No doubts?"

"None whatsoever."

Now it was Gemma's turn to suck in a sharp breath. "Whatever happens, I'm here for you."

"Thanks, friend." That brought a well of tears to Molly's eyes.

"Come on. Let's go face the troops." Gemma groaned as she hooked her arm through Molly. "Your mom wasn't like this before. What happened on that trip, I wonder, to make her so—"

"Forceful? Unvarnished?" Molly agreed, each step closer brought a little more dread in her belly. "If we're lucky it's just a phase. Daddy's still all about money and expenses. The ingrained accountant. I think he's relieved they came back early and saved some."

"Loose ends? That's got to be it. We need to get them back to work and fast."

Molly chuckled. "Now who's running whose life?"

"Well, it's about time!" Molly's mother waited at the top

of the hill with her hands on her hips while holding something.

"Just catching up." Icicles stabbed Molly in her gut now. "I like that new powder-blue blouse on you, Mom." Distract. Dodge.

"Come along. You've kept us waiting long enough already." She half turned to head back.

"W-wait, Mom." She quivered when her mother turned back with raised eyebrows. Why did she have to do that? The stern mom slash teacher look that always left Molly shaking lived on.

"You're dawdling again."

"Come on. We finally snagged a table for five." Her father waved an arm for them to come as he stood outside the coffee shop.

Sean stood slightly behind their dad, shaking his head and shrugging his shoulders. That was his way of silently telling her he wasn't on board, but had been roped in unwillingly.

Molly glanced from him to her dad, to her mom, and then to Gemma. The closest people in her world… This reminded her of that summer, nearly six years ago, almost two months after Adam had left and she still wallowed. These people had called her downstairs from her bedroom and circled around her.

It was not pretty then.

Somehow, it would be worse now. Her parents wanted her to live the life they expected her to—good daughter, teacher, marry the proper guy, good wife, have the required one boy and one girl, good mom—not the life she wanted.

She trembled now, facing down her mother. "An intervention, really?"

"Apparently you need one." Her mother flicked the paper, tapping the folded back page. "It's terrible what that boy is doing to you again."

Molly's middle clutched. *Adam.* She reached for the paper thrust at her. With shaky hands, Molly dropped her gaze to the blurry print. She blinked a few times to read the glaring headline and subtext. *Has Love Returned to Cupid's Corner? Can high school sweethearts get their second chance at love?*

However, the two large grainy accompanying pictures sucked the breath out of Molly's lungs. They were the ones Adam had taken of them on the boat, right after he hoisted himself back in—wet, smiling up at the camera with her red hair splayed out, and their heads touching and the one where they had turned to kiss each other.

That one she knew was supposed to be the fake reunion one. But the other…the kissing one…

He didn't! No, it couldn't be.

Then she recalled Bernard barging in on them at her studio and taking photos.

With a more discerning eye, Molly noted the angle and the framing—the computer screen behind where they had stood.

A well of relief rushed through her. Adam hadn't sold them out.

"You should read the rest of the article. It's

quite…interesting." Her mother's tone had Molly looking up.

It was the triumphant look on her mother's face that clued Molly in to the gist of the article.

She handed the paper back. "Why don't you save me the time and tell me, Mom?"

Her mother bristled, standing straighter.

She turned to Sean and Molly's dad. "Go on. We'll be there shortly." When they did follow along, she faced Molly again. "Gemma, why don't you join the fellas, too?"

Her best friend brushed it aside. "Don't be silly. They can catch up some."

Thank you, Gem, for standing by me.

"Well, if you must then…Bernard interviewed *him*—"

"Adam. His name is *Adam*." Molly smiled tightly.

Her mother cleared her throat. "He bought the place to give back and invest in the community. Really? Him? Reuniting with you was, so he says, a gift he never thought he'd ever get. What a load! And he apparently is here for only a few weeks and gone again."

Yeah, I suspected that before he even told me. And he never covered that up. "He has a thriving business. And he's going to college."

For the first time, her mother lost some of her composure. "Col-lege, you say?"

"Great grades, too." Molly raised her chin.

All that tamped down rumbling a few weeks ago had dissipated. However, there were lingering pockets of heat that were now drifting up and into her chest, pressing there.

"It doesn't matter. He's already showed you who he was. Haven't you learned anything from that horrible time?"

Everything stung, trying to climb up and out her throat.

Molly gulped in air. "Mom, I can't do this."

"That's what I've been trying to tell you, dear. You can't have that boy back in your world ever again."

"Not that. He's a man now. He's done well for himself and his family." The words defending Adam rolled out. "But he's not what I...need to...talk to you about. It's me." Those, about herself, she had to drag out from her depths.

"Ah, so you've come to your senses. You were supposed to apply for my temporary teaching position to cover for me while I was gone on my sabbatical. Now, I go back for a year in the fall, you substitute teach at the high school, and apply for the following school year to take over my spot when I plan to retire."

"You're not listening."

"Really, you've just dragged this all out for nothing. It's a good, secure position. You just have to be firm with the students—"

"Mom." It sounded awful and made her queasy to think about.

"We'll toughen you up some."

Anxiety bubbled up. "I can't do that."

"Don't be ridiculous. I'll fill out the forms for you tonight."

Molly's throat closed up. "No." It squeaked out. "No!" That one shot out and dropped in the air.

"Wh-what did you say?" Her mother's jaw slacked and

her eyes grew wide.

"I don't want your life. It works for you. Not *me*. I'm different. I'm creative, not structured like that. I'd be bored to death." Molly gained strength. "So, I don't live up to what you want. I still love you and you still love me. Sometimes that has to be enough, all right?"

Molly blinked back hot, stinging tears.

Stepping forward, she embraced her mother. "You can do it, Mom. Just wrap your arms around me." She smiled when her mom did with robotic moves and tension in her entire body. "Relax, Mom. I'm not a failure. I'm actually happier than I've ever been."

Her mother's stance softened, her arms were not as stiff.

"Hey, look there's some things I can teach you, too." She chuckled through her tears. "You don't have to run my life, try to arrange it, or plan it just so I'll have some direction and avoid pain. Whatever happens to me, I'll be all right. Promise." Deep down, Molly knew that to be true and a flood of relief washed over her.

She turned her head and kissed her mother's soft cheek before pulling away.

"My…little girl." Her mother's chin wobbled.

"Is all grown up. Sorry about that." She put an arm around Gemma's shoulder, hugging her to her side. "Mom, you'll have to wait for Gemma and Sean to give you grand-babies."

"Hey, let's not go from zero to a hundred." Gemma nudged Molly with her knee.

"Why not, Gem? Welcome to my world." Molly chuckled, feeling lighter and freer than she had in a very long time, if ever.

Only she had no idea what to do about Adam anymore...

Chapter Nineteen

"READY, LARSON?" MOLLY stopped in front of him, grinning.

Somehow, he could see only her; all the crazy-busy activity surrounding them slowly slid away. The loud noises from the trucks coming and going muted, the hammering too, and orders his foreman barked out to the crew faded into the background.

Everything condensed to this moment with Molly and him, in their own little world. Again.

How did that happen with them? How had he forgotten this part—this intense awareness?

Keeping it on the friend side outwardly hadn't changed a darn thing on the inside for him.

And the soft, sweet kiss she'd given him in the field while taking photos had floored him so he didn't know up from down anymore.

Reaching out, Adam tipped her girlie hardhat back so he could see her breathtaking blue eyes—warm and sparkling. *His* breath stayed trapped in his lungs. A fusion of tingles ran up his spine. She'd owned his reaction to her from the start.

She's doing it again. "Enjoying yourself?"

"Maybe."

Was she flirting? He liked it. He thought Bernard's highly speculative, human-interest newspaper article on them and the venue would drive a wedge between them. Apparently, with just a grimace and shoving the paper at him earlier, she'd ended the matter on her own terms. "What's this adventure you're taking me on again?"

"It's business. And it's a little surprise."

"Three hours tops."

"If you say so…" The way her voice trailed away spoke volumes.

This didn't appear to be a simple furniture shopping expedition. "I'll let my foreman and Pickens know. Meet you at my truck."

She gave him a jaunty salute, pivoted on her heel—holding her camera in place so it wouldn't swing—and marched off.

Adam grinned, shaking his head at her cute little walk and her attitude turnaround. Thankfully, she'd put aside her reservations on lending a hand with this enormous project.

He had just over three weeks now to pull this together before the first pretend wedding—their intro to the industry. *Down to the wire.*

Ten minutes later, he rolled to a stop at the entrance. "Which way, angel?"

"Pit stop first." She dragged her hand from the crown of her head, sliding it down the long red strands. Then she fingered combed her hair, loosening it.

A sharp ache arrowed through his gut. She was so dang sexy when she did that and she had no idea then or now. "Ah, what again?" *Pit stop?*

"Our helpers for the day. Not quite hitchhikers, mind you." She pointed to her left. "That way."

"Back to town? The more you talk, the more confused I get." He eased onto the empty two-lane road; his crew had halted for a much-needed break. "No other clues for me?"

"We could play twenty questions?"

"Or not."

He rather liked her playful nature, something he'd seldom witnessed while they were in high school. She'd been too quiet and shy to let herself shine through. He liked the changes in his Molly.

"Who's your favorite person?"

"You." It came out without a thought.

It was true. Molly always had been. She made him feel ten feet tall, even away from the football field and all his accolades in sports. Those didn't matter to her. He did.

Molly stilled, frowning as she held his gaze for a brief second before he returned his attention to the road. "I guess I never knew that."

"I should have told you."

"Well…" She sighed. "I didn't, either. Talk much. About us. You were my fave, too." She shrugged. "Then Gemma."

"Of course. You two were thick as thieves then." He tried to smooth the ragged edges to his pulse. Why hadn't they simply talked back then? *Because we were just kids.*

He came back to the here and now. "You left me hanging? Helper?"

She giggled. "Two actually. The very best experts in the county, I'd say."

"First it's confusion now double talk. Literally."

"You still haven't learned patience, have you? You want everything right here right now." Her voice grew heavy and slow, like she'd hit a realization.

Adam blew out a breath in the suddenly thick air. Funny how she powered down her window a few inches and sucked in the warm May breeze.

"I wanted you, Molly." His voice came out low and husky. *Still do.* "I wanted to slide into a great life with you. Full speed ahead in five seconds flat."

"You, too?" She tried to chuckle, but it came out on a puff. "We were so unrealistic back then. Hardships? We ignored the possibilities. Pretty immature of us, don't you think?"

"That's a nice way to put it." He hesitated a moment, driving by the wheat and corn fields and acre after acre of woods, winding down the hilltop. "I didn't have a backup plan after I didn't make it into college. All or nothing…"

Molly gasped, jerking her head to look at him as he braked at a stop sign, the metal slightly squealing. "Adam! You couldn't have all, so you choose nothing."

"Really selfish of me." He couldn't share *nothing* with her; she deserved better than he could give her—a bleak present and maybe even bleaker future.

"Or…selfless. I'm not quite sure which one yet."

Stunned wonder chased across her features and then the shutters came down.

Silence strummed between them.

"You chose for us, ripping that Band-Aid off."

He couldn't gauge her at the moment and that surprised him. Years ago, he could read her different moods—every movement, every word, every nuance—shy, quiet, and reserved ones, but still very telling hiding behind her camera. Now, not so much. "Moll—"

"That way. To Vine Street."

"You're not asking to be dropped off at your shop, are you?"

She shook her head. "Our hotshot crew, remember? We're picking them up there."

"Whatever the lady says." He turned the steering wheel in that direction and drove on.

They traveled through light traffic into town for a few miles.

Out of the blue, Molly turned to him in a swift, sure motion. "You. Did. The right thing." She swallowed hard and then turned back to the window, blinking rapidly.

The tangled knot buried deep in his gut unhitched a rung or two. It had been far too long since he'd had any relief over leaving her that awful, heart-wrenching day.

She'd given him more than a crumb. Now he had to learn how to forgive himself for hurting her…

MOLLY SHOOK FROM the inside out. She clutched the door handle on Adam's truck, her knuckles tight and white.

Every time she drew in a breath she ached from her burning lungs to every fiber of her being.

Why hadn't she'd seen it before—without the starry-eyes and then the blanket of shame?

Adam Larson protected her. Once scorned for his humble background and then revered for his moves on the football field, he earned respect. It stayed attached to him and anyone he welcomed into his small, nearly nonexistent circle.

From the day he'd shoved aside a group of bullies surrounding Molly when they were in junior high, through joining her at the school lunch table when Gemma was out sick that first time, to sitting beside Molly in classes, to their sophomore year when he finally asked her out, all through their dating time, and, most of all, when he put the brakes on them—calling off the wedding a week before.

He'd wanted so much more for her. And if he couldn't give it then he'd walk away.

Only it had torn her heart apart, ripping it to shreds.

Now, she sensed it had done the same for him.

Because he loved me.

"You okay?" The words tumbled from her numb lips.

She stared blindly out the window, watching the flashes of lush green grass and fields switch to sidewalk, the hill, and this side of the pond as they slowed down on the outskirts of town.

"I'm not sure."

"That's an honest answer." She released the trapped air in her chest by slow degrees.

At least they were being real. And raw. Where would they go from here, though?

"Ah, navigator?" He inched to a crawl.

She craned her neck to scan the pedestrians nearby on the cross street. "Turn onto Vine and pull to the curb."

"I thought we weren't—" Adam must have seen the sweet, older couple waving. "Mr. and Mrs. Valentine!" He grinned.

"The one and only." She smiled, adoring the charming grandparents of her best friend.

In moments, after idling there, Molly hopped out to greet them.

Grams rushed to her, embracing her. "Molly, it's so wonderful to see you again, sweetheart!"

"You, too, Grams. You give the best hugs ever." Growing up, Molly loved visiting the couple at their antiques shop, pitching in, working there part-time as a teenager with her bestie, and made to feel like part of the close-knit, loving Valentine family.

She chuckled when Gramps hugged them both. "Our Molly."

Pulling back slightly, she glanced at them and turned to Adam, tilting her head for him to join them. "Look who I brought you?"

"Finally! I get to see him." Grams pressed her hands to her cheeks. "Adam, honey!" She went to him as he came forward and then reached up to gather him close. "You're a sight for sore eyes, dear."

Gramps followed behind, grabbing a hand and shaking it, and then giving him a half hug over his wife's shorter frame. "Great to see you, son."

"You, too. Both of you." Adam seemed a little shell-shocked at the warm greeting as he stepped back.

Molly's heart squeezed. He hadn't had that welcome since returning. Part of it had to do with her. No one should judge him by her pain over the breakup. Hopefully, this venture would right some wrongs for Adam.

"Ready?" She popped open the back door on the quad truck.

"Am I? I could hardly do a thing after you called this morning, dear." Grams tugged Gramps to follow her. "Now, honey, you'll have to push when I tell you."

"Here, let me." Adam assisted Grams to the step-up running board below the edge of the door. "Grab the bar above you, Mrs. V."

"Got it! Heave ho!" She yanked herself up and plopped down in the seat. She turned to them, laughing. "I still got it!"

"Yes, you do." Adam grinned.

Molly tried to look away, honestly, she did. However, he captured her gaze at that moment and her pulse leapt.

He stilled.

Her knees wobbled.

Adam came to her, assisting her up to the passenger seat—at one point her back skimmed his chest—and they both sucked in a sharp breath.

She settled in as he rounded the truck, making certain Gramps was in and secured before he jumped in behind the wheel.

"Ready?" He looked over at her and she wasn't certain if she could answer him.

For what? When all this is over and you leave me again? No, never ready for that.

"Hit the road, Adam!" Grams leaned forward, patting him on the shoulder and then gave him directions out of town. She pulled back. "Sweetheart, hand me my purse, will you?"

"The weight set?" Gramps's voice held a smile.

"A girl's gotta be prepared."

Molly glanced back, watching Grams pull out one thing after the other—piling it on the seat between her and Gramps as she went.

"Here they are!" Grams drew out a plastic-wrapped stack of homemade treats. "Heart-shaped sugar cookies, Adam, with the little bit of pale pink glaze on top. Your favorite."

"How did you remember?" He shook his head.

"Me? I always remember my kids and what they liked."

The way she said *my kids* had Adam jerking his head to gaze at Molly for a split, heart-melting second. There was a well of gratitude mixed with wonder shining in his eyes.

Yeah, Adam, you were always one of us. You always belonged to us, to me. You just didn't know it or accept it then.

Chapter Twenty

HOURS LATER AND five delicious cookies consumed, Adam trudged behind Molly and an overly energetic Grams. Surely they'd found enough tables and chairs and decorations to fill a warehouse by now. At least the back of his truck held some pieces covered with his handy tarp. He'd arranged for the various other items to be delivered to the barn or picked up by some of his guys this week.

"Told you. You need to conserve, Adam." Gramps chuckled from a rocking chair in the current flea market shop, sipping a bottle of water.

"How do you do this?" Adam plopped down on a nearby seat, losing sight of the ladies as they rushed along another aisle, chattering excitedly. "How do they?"

"My sweetie thrives on this. Mind you, she's got more time on her hands now that we closed up Valentine's At Vine…"

That nugget tugged at Adam. "Not putting anything else in there?"

"After the construction and scaffolding come down for good? Hope so. Miss that spot where everyone stopped by to visit, buy a piece here and there, and catch up. Like a brief moment in Cupid's Corner history all running right through our front door, so to speak."

It settled in the deepest part of Adam. He wanted to keep that alive, too. "I may need a place in town. Nothing full-time. A side thing that shouldn't take up too much time most of the year, just during the high season. For potential customers to gather information about the wedding and event venue—Molly handed over the details to my assistant and she's having brochures made—make appointments to come see it, and things like that. Something you and Mrs. V. would be interested in?"

Adam spoke off the cuff, trying to give them something, while figuring out how he'd handle the traffic to and from the private venue. It would be easier in town, close to Molly and her studio she'd keep there for the time being, too. He'd have to work out all the specifics with her.

"The hub? My sweetie would love that. Like a welcome center." He sighed, pushing one foot to rock with.

"There you are, dear." Grams came up behind him, patting Adam on the back. "I think we hit the motherlode."

He groaned.

Molly, standing nearby, giggled.

The sweet sound caused him to smile and look up. In wonder, he watched her suck in a sharp breath and his head began to spin.

Long ago, he thought he could be her everything. He'd tried. Until he failed. Now, he just wanted to give her everything he could. Every last thing. Except him. Because guys like him—working guys—didn't believe in dreams ever coming true. That was a fantasy.

She was beautiful and amazing and so out of reach. Still.

IN SPITE OF the brewing storm with loud thunderclaps and streaks of violent lightning slashing the night sky, Molly fought the sleepiness on the ride home after the long day of treasure hunting with the Valentines.

Or was that the big steak dinner Adam had treated them all to after finding the spectacle, all unique twenty-one crystal chandeliers stored away in the old lighting company tucked behind the flea market shop?

Adam eased up on the pedal and flicked on his windshield wipers at the sudden splash of rain dumping down.

Resting against the headrest, she rolled her head to stare at Adam as Grams chattered in back, delight filling her voice at the new plans she and Gramps were cooking up. Adam glanced at her, smiling, knowing what an amazing day they'd shared.

She liked his idea of the sweet older couple's shop included in the venture—a vital location in the heart of Cupid's Corner—while giving them a much-needed purpose to contribute to the town.

Her heart swelled with pride and admiration for Adam.

Deep down, she realized this dream would all be over in a matter of weeks. He'd be back to running his entire business full-time and she'd be leaping into more adventurous photography—natural, fun, and memorial—poses at meaningful places along with numerous weddings—still a little scary to think of—booked for this summer. Also, she'd oversee the event center. For now.

The only thing she had left was to find a different place to live. She needed her space from her well-meaning family. Could she really move into the carriage house when he left like he'd offered?

Memories of him being there might be more difficult to get over him this time. Yeah, like that would happen in this lifetime.

Still, it was time for Molly to fly the coop and spread her wings.

Only, part of her ached down to her toes at the coming loss of Adam…

ADAM SLOWED AS they came to the outskirts of town, the rain coming hard and steady. "Home, Grams and Gramps?"

"How lovely of you, Adam." Grams reached out and patted his shoulder. "Such a dear boy."

The closer he got, the more his cell phone pinged again and again. "And I think we have cell service back. Must be text and voice mail—"

Sirens sliced through the air.

Adam watched the volunteer firefighters whizz by in their personal vehicles and flashing lights on top one after the other, the speed of them shaking his truck.

"Oh my!" Grams said what they all felt. "It must be a big one for all these cars."

His chest tightened as he powered down his window, rain pelting against his exposed face. "Smoke. Can you see anything on your side, Moll?" Something in Cupid's Corner was burning.

She sat up straighter, ready to follow along when her phone rang. Grabbing for it, she hit the speaker button. "Gem?"

"Moll, it's Sean. Gemma's driving us. Where are you?"

As he rounded a bend, Adam slammed on the brakes, reaching out to stop Molly from lurching forward. His blood ran cold. "Fire. The barn!" The flames licked high, but the plume of smoke swirled even higher from across the pond.

"No, Adam!" Molly's shocked voice mixed with the Valentines' cries. "Sean, we're headed there now."

"Meet you…" His phone died.

"Pickens!" Shivers went up Adam's spine and through his body. "He's got to be okay. That's all that matters. Moll, call him. Hold on, everyone!" He didn't wait for answers. Adam maneuvered his truck around, making an illegal U-turn, and then floored it, the contents in the back shifting and jarring together. Thankfully, the rain let up to a pitter-patter and his headlights sliced through the dark roads.

He knew the red taillights of the firefighters' vehicles were headed to the fire station to get the truck first. Some would haul it to the barn, but they didn't know the place like he did. Or Pickens.

In the back of his mind, Adam hoped the old man didn't

charge in and try to put out the fire and that he was safe…

ADAM PARKED ACROSS the street in the soggy field. The rain had stopped on the hill, but everything was still slick with water. "Stay here!" He bolted, hoping his running back days in high school still served him. The distance proved well over the hundred yards of a football field. The ghost-like, darkened white house appeared in front of Adam through the smoky haze.

Maybe the storm had knocked out the lights.

"Pickens! Pickens!"

No one shouted back.

Up ahead, gray smoke clung and rolled, catching in Adam's raw throat and burning lungs. Flames licked higher, snapping and crackling in the night sky. Wood creaked and splintered deep inside the barn.

Sirens coming up the hill filled the air, making it harder for Adam to hear close by.

"Pickens!" He came upon the old beat-up truck, pounded on the metal. It pinged back. Cupping his hands and looking in, Adam found it empty.

With his heart in his throat, he jerked around at the unmistakable sound of rushing water. He watched in shock as the old man stood too close to the structure with a garden hose pointed inside.

Adam raced to him. "Get back!" He wrestled for the water line and tried to shove the solid man away. "Meet the firetrucks at the entrance. Direct them back."

"Not leaving!" He picked up a nearby filled bucket. "Lightning struck. Started the fire."

"I'll do it. Cover the flames from that side." Adam lurched for the bucket, grabbed it, and then rushed to the threshold. His eyes burned. His stomach knotted at the sight—caved-in roof on that side and fire roared and ate up the wall. He flung the bucket of water, knowing it was a teardrop when they needed a flood.

He had no idea how many times he went back before the firefighters nearly tackled him and dragged him away.

"Come on, man. We don't need a rescue here." The captain convinced him.

With Pickens shaking by his side, Adam stood far back, watching the skilled volunteer firemen do what they did best. Hoses from three angles sprayed down on the flames. Hisses and bellows of gray smoke followed.

Sometime before dawn, and still in a daze even after a shot of oxygen, Adam watched Molly breaking away from her family, the Valentines, most of the townspeople, and through the police barricade to rush down the long driveway. Flashes of lights went off as Bernard took snapshots with his old, clunky camera.

"Adam!" Molly, with tears streaming down her face, ran the last few yards. "You're safe." She flung herself into his arms, holding him tight.

"Molly." He crushed her to him, burying his head in her neck, inhaling the sweet scent of her. Anything to drag him back from the smoke-laced air and to sanity again.

She kissed him on his cheek, his chin, and then his mouth.

Her sweetness nearly undid him. "I'm sorry, angel."

"What? Why? You and Mr. Pickens are all right."

He pulled back enough to look down into her eyes. Defeat dragged him down, knowing he'd just lost everything for good now. Especially his Molly. "I wanted to give you a dream. There's only a nightmare left."

Chapter Twenty-One

HOURS RAN INTO days and then a week. Molly still shook every time she thought of how close Adam had been to that fire.

And his hollow eyes…

They haunted her.

She tried to contact him, but he refused her calls. Comfort? Yeah, no. He'd been short and firm after his disclosure on losing the wedding venue.

Like it was his fault. Or he felt to blame.

The fire marshal released the property this morning so she was certain Adam was back there now.

The bell over her shop door rang. She jerked her head up, hoping it was Adam. No such luck. Hope plunged.

Pasting on a smile, she watched the triplets' mom maneuver them through the door—*who's dragging who now*—and into the space. Their laughs and cries sliced through the normally quiet air.

"Hey, girls!" Molly came around, stooped down, and scooped them up for hugs. They squeezed her neck. "Choking. Must work on that."

They giggled and then wiggled away, going straight for her new white cubbies filled with all sorts of accessories and the low hanging rod with costumes on them. Yeah, she'd had a lot of time on her hands this last week…

She hefted herself to her feet and wiped her hands on her jeans. "Need do-overs?"

"No. We were in the area and just wanted to stop by to take a look at their poster-size photos in your windows—they love them—and to thank you for the amazing pictures of the girls. Their grandmas loved them for Mother's Day gifts, just like you suggested."

"I'm glad." She noted the woman's relaxed, calm stance. "Things improved?"

Raising a hand to her head, she nodded and then chuck-led. "Spacewise, no. But stresswise, yes. I sat my husband down and we had the best heart-to-heart talk. We'd rather have him home with us than off working all those hours for a bigger, more expensive house—because without him it wouldn't really be a home, now, would it? Strange how we were projecting what we thought the other wanted but neither of us really want that chaotic, unfulfilling life with me stuck at home cleaning and him stuck at work missing us." She sighed. "It's simple and perfect and complicated and imperfect just the way it is."

Molly laughed. "That sounds about right. I'm happy for you."

Less than five minutes later, Molly waved off the little family. The mother's words struck her hard. *Projecting what we thought the other wanted…*

It made her think of Adam and her.

They'd had unspoken expectations of what they and their marriage should be. Or maybe what others expected it to be and they'd have to live up to it…and never thought they could.

Adam, we were setting ourselves up for failure…then. I am now, too.

Because second chances didn't happen to someone like her. And in order for a hopeless romantic to survive, she had to give up on the crazy dream of having a picture-perfect life.

THIRTY MINUTES LATER, Molly eased off the gas pedal and turned into the barn driveway. The big house had black streaks along the planks, marked from the smoky haze last week.

Everything looked different, empty, and forlorn now.

Gone were the numerous trucks, equipment, and supplies from the yard. The absent, once-busy crew sank in, too; they had been all reassigned to other, busy worksites. Even the high expectance and anticipation dissipated to leave a flat, dull feeling behind.

Defeat. Despair.

Heavy arid scent hung in the air like a cloud too heavy to lift.

She slowly approached, the tires crunching along what was left of the gravel, imprinted and torn up from the big, thick firetruck wheels and vehicles there that night and most likely since.

Seeing Adam's truck caused her to swallow hard. *He's here.*

A tiny bolt of shock raced through her at the familiar car parked on the other side of his.

"Mom and Dad? What are they doing here?" Thoughts of them confronting Adam churned in her mind and low in her belly. "Hasn't he had to deal with enough?"

On shaky limbs, Molly walked to the barn where muted voices came. She didn't dare look at the beloved carriage house where he stayed and she'd hoped one day to take over. Not likely anymore.

Rumors in town swirled of Adam selling the property now...

But, thankfully, the carriage house had been saved. Only minor smoke damage was reported. And she refused to give the adorable bridal she-shed more than a quick, longing look. Also, grateful for it being spared.

"Frankly, if you've come to gloat, I don't want you here. As you can see it's a wash. Nothing to see." Adam's voice echoed, pulling Molly closer.

She halted at the wide open door entrance, peering inside. Her heart lurched to her throat. Fire, smoke, and water damage greeted her. All those weeks of work ruined. *Poor Adam.*

"The structure held up." Her mother pointed out the obvious.

"Old bones." Adam bit out. "There's more, but is it really necessary to go over?"

"So, just like that you're scrapping it?" She could almost see her father's mind calculating the cost as he walked in a semicircle, gazing up and around.

"Insurance covered most."

"What about our daughter?" Her mother's voice reached out from the other side of the barn.

Molly stepped forward, longing to hear more. She counted the steps, five, six, seven… *Would she have to jump in if her parents got out of hand?*

"This is what you wanted, isn't it? Me out of the picture, no pun intended." It came out on a low growl.

"Of course." Her mother didn't disguise the truth.

"She didn't know her own mind." Her father's back was toward Molly.

"Is that what you thought?" Adam jammed his hands in his jeans pockets, pacing. "She's funny and smart and incredibly talented. You didn't give her her due."

"Or you yours." Those few words dropped like an explosion from her mother.

Molly's belly clenched. What were they talking about? And why now?

"Why didn't you ever tell her, Adam?" The hoarse question hung between them.

"What, that her mother—our class advisor—hated the thought of her daughter marrying beneath her that she purposely refused to allow my English class extra credit work to count toward my grade so I'd lose my scholarship?"

A gasp tore through the air. *Her* gasp. Molly watched as they pivoted toward her, various stages of shock registering on their features. "Mom?"

The guilty flush said it all.

"You did that." It stuck in her dry throat. Molly swallowed hard several times. Evidence of his great college grades flashed through her mind. "How could you try to ruin Adam's life like that?"

"I—I did it for you, honey. I wanted better for you." Her mother brushed away a tear.

"No." She shook her head. "Not for me. For *you*." The triplets' mother's words rang in her ears. *Expectations.* "So you wouldn't be embarrassed by Adam and where he came from."

"Let's not get all upset now, Molly." Her father held up his hands in an attempt to soothe her like he often did. "We wouldn't want you to get sick."

"Excuse me, but I think I have just cause for being ticked off." The bubbling anger blurred the edges of her vision. "I'm not fragile or weak. Sure I cry when I hurt. I wallow when I'm in deep pain. It's called emotions. You're scared of them."

Her parents glanced at each other and looked away quickly.

That hit the target; they didn't want to get all messy and mushy and lose control of who they were or what they pretended to stand for.

"We're not… We, all right, *I* wanted you to get an education first and find someone at college, someone more appropriate." Her mother's choked voice bounced off the bare walls. "Your father knew nothing of what I did, until I confessed after the fire last week. I mean, how much did Adam have to lose this…time. I came to apologize to Adam."

Her father coughed. "And offer our help somehow. I don't know, make up for our terrible mistakes."

Molly blinked, focusing on Adam coming toward her. For the first time, she saw all the things he'd been hiding from her, most of all the anguish in his raw, tortured gaze. "You didn't trust *me*." Hot tears came. "Not to handle the truth. How were we going to have a chance if you kept the most important things from me? You're just as bad as they were, are. What, did I mean so little to you?"

"I wanted to protect you." His voice cracked.

"Funny, it didn't work out that way." She ached with betrayal all the way down to her bones. Had anyone ever been truly honest with her? "We're done, right? No, don't answer." Molly sucked in a ragged breath. "I can make my own decisions even if no one thinks I'm capable of them. Yeah, it's over."

A slash of agony crossed his face. Molly turned, knowing that must be how she looked at the moment. This was what he wanted, right? An end to them once and for all. Because why else would he come back and try to ease the burden on his mind? Well, he'd done a great job at it this time. Curling her hands into fists, she willed herself to take a step and then another away from him and what her foolish mind screamed for.

There were no second chances. Not for her.

"The world." Adam's words didn't make sense. "The answer to your question is, you meant the world to me, Molly. You still do."

All right, just rip my heart out of my chest for a second time, why don't you, Adam Larson?

Chapter Twenty-Two

"I NEVER TOOK you for a quitter, son." Pickens's raspy voice cut through the dark interior down below. The scratchy sound came from the smoke inhalation he'd suffered trying to save the place.

"You're the only one who thinks so then." Adam stood on the sturdy second-floor rafter at the open barn door. This was the view he'd dreamed of for six long years, recalling Molly beside him. He glanced at the frame and then reached out and traced their initials he'd carved there back then.

"Got a lot of people asking questions about the reconstruction."

"Tell them to stop asking."

"Well, about that…" He must have walked closer; now his words weren't so far away. "That Mrs. Valentine has a list going around for people to sign up."

Grams. "Nice lady. Makes great sugar cookies, too." Everything inside Adam hurt at losing this—no, losing Molly again. Excruciating pain ripped through his chest. Again.

"Don't you want to know what the list is for?"

"Not really, but I guess you're going to tell me."

The old man's laugh turned to a cough. "Volunteers. Yep, seems like the good people of Cupid's Corner want that wedding venue and event center you promised them."

Adam stilled. In the aftermath of the fire, he'd made the difficult decision to put a halt to construction. Not this summer. Not with only two weeks left before the first wedding, well, opening introduction to the industry people. Then when Molly gazed at him with such raw pain and betrayal, Adam didn't have it in him to do this without her.

This was her dream. Well, the bigger and better one than when they were engaged and she decided to become a wedding photographer. He'd added the rest when he found the farm up for sale nearly three months ago. A gift he could give her. One for a lifetime…

"They have faith in you, Adam."

That surprised him. Maybe it was left over from his high school playing days when Sean handed him the football, Adam tucked it securely in his arms, booked it to the end zone, and then scored the winning touchdown.

"Said they want a good hometown boy like you to show everyone what you're made of—and what the town is made of, too. They're behind you all the way. Always have been. You just didn't know it."

After all he'd put Molly through, they still wanted to support him? Adam blew out a heavy breath.

"What should I tell them, son?"

TEN LONG DAYS and Molly rode the edge of sanity. Well, just barely. It didn't help that the townspeople talked of nothing else than how the wedding venue was coming along.

They pitched in and powered on, helping Adam clear away the debris, offer reclaimed lumber from their own places, and flat-out lent a hand in most everything that had to be done. Sometimes, traffic backed up to get to the hill in different shifts.

Even her parents were making meals for his crew and delivering them. Her mom barely cooked. How crazy was that?

Sean gave advice on the architecture when needed. Gemma found plenty of history books of the region at her library to give input on the age and look of the building and surroundings.

The sweet Valentines—Grams, Gramps, and Gemma's folks—provided coordinating, redone salvaged pieces for the interior, and lots of good old-fashioned work.

Molly refused the checks Adam's company sent her, well, all but the first five-figure one she'd agreed on in the beginning. It was more than enough for what she'd done. The rest she'd hadn't earned and didn't want. They finally got the message and stopped sending them.

And every few days, as Molly worked feverishly to avoid the commotion and blunt the heartache, Mr. Pickens would call just like her cell phone ID told her now.

She warred inside at picking it up. "I give up." She blinked away the burn in her eyes from gazing at her computer screen for hours on end to get the right image. *Keep kidding yourself.* "Hey, Mr. Pickens. How are you feeling?"

"Right as rain, Miss Molly. Voice is improving every day, too. Now, just between you and me, he won't be back until late tomorrow."

That was their secret code.

"Hear me?"

"Y-yes."

"He's got some business things to take care of out-of-town and such. I'll see you at dawn, right?"

Everything tugged inside her. She'd done this twice before and darn it if she couldn't help herself.

"Right?"

"Put the coffee on for me, well, herbal tea, I'm still off caffeine. Why, I have no idea."

He chuckled. "Will do, miss."

MOLLY GASPED. THE bridal waiting she-shed looked like something out of her dreams. White painted walls, the warm wood stained floors, curved stairs led up to the small room where brides would change into their beautiful gowns. And all around in the lower room were dainty, girly vanities, tables, and chairs. Every detail from refurbished lanterns and light fixtures, to French doors, to just the perfect little patio with pink chairs to lounge in captured and delighted her.

"Mighty nice, isn't it?" Mr. Pickens stood back just outside the door, allowing her to take the photos.

She took dozens of them, although, she wondered how

Adam had pulled off the incredible task of placing each specific piece she'd spoken about weeks ago.

"Adam did the entire place. He wouldn't hear of anyone else touching it. Finished yesterday right before he left."

He listened to my dream.

With a shaky hand, she raised her camera again, taking different angles and then slowly climbing the stairs. The cute little room nestled at the top held the long full-length mirror with white trim around the oblong edges. Two chairs were here and a delicate curtained-off area near the mannequin form stood nearby. There was even a little balcony. She peeked out, catching the image of the barn as a bride would see it with hope and excitement of what was to come.

When she was done, Molly stepped down on shaky legs. She sank on the fifth stair up and gazed out the open door.

Mr. Pickens peeked his head in. "There's more."

She shook her head, wondering if she were in a dream. "More?"

"The groom's room." He tilted his head toward the carriage house. "Adam redid the lower level. Very masculine."

Curiosity tugged at her. "What has he come up with now, I wonder?" Excitement bubbled up inside her at the prospect. He'd stunned her with this gorgeous little place.

The older man matched her steps as she walked across the long yard, now almost fully landscaped. "The complete opposite to the bride's. Dark wood and even a pool table. But you can see it for yourself. Landscapers finish up this afternoon. See where they cut back the trees, hacked away the dead shrubs, added the hydrangea bushes all around, and, down there, planted the lilacs."

Molly halted in midstride and blinked as she looked around, unable to find them. "Lilacs?"

"More to come on the outside of the bride shack. I guess we have to come up with a better name than that. Purple ones to go on either side of the little porch. Adam made sure of that. The rest of them are down near the pond where Adam had a nice stone firepit put in with chairs all around. You know, for families or even the guys after fishing some. There's a path with the lilacs on both sides. Must love those bushes because he sure did order a lot—mostly the purple, some pink, and some white."

She barely let him finish before she raced toward the wide stretch of freshly mowed grass between the barn and carriage house.

"To your right…" Mr. Pickens's voice carried.

Following his directions, Molly found the path about four feet in width winding down and branching out to an open heart-shaped area. The full grown lilac bushes swayed gently in the breeze with sun-bleached stones lining each side of the long path.

She took a few steps, gasped at the magnificent row of plump flowers in brilliant colors, and then fell to her knees.

"Adam."

Tears smarted the backs of her eyes. She grabbed for her camera, taking a few pictures out of focus because she was crying harder now. "You did this for me. My favorites."

Her heart swelled. "I remember your promise to me then…and you've made it come true. Even better."

"YOU MUST. I insist." Molly's mother gave Adam that raised eyebrow.

He shivered. "Really? You're trying to use that high school teacher look on me?" Taking two steps to the side, he was disappointed when she did the same, still confronting him.

"It's working, isn't it?"

"Seems like it." He eyed the black tux she held draped over her arm. She wore a champagne-colored silk suit and had her hair done up. She'd really taken this over the top for someone who once didn't want him around. "Why does the owner of the place have to wear a tuxedo?" *For his wedding that won't ever happen?* That realization punched him right in the gut. Again.

Molly. I miss you.

Tomorrow, he'd leave for good.

First, he endured the pressure, the details falling into place, the hired help setting up the last of the tables, the makeshift kitchen buzzing with activity, and the ever-present townspeople who he'd decided were invited to the industry showing turned to celebration for all their hard work and effort. Only he couldn't bring himself to feel the measure of glee and delight they did.

Standing in the refurbished barn caused Adam to stare in wonder at his surroundings. Without the kind, good-hearted people of Cupid's Corner he'd have never gotten it finished on time for this—opening day.

The chandeliers Molly and Mrs. V. selected were lit and worked perfectly in the area as did the round tables with the blush-pink silk cloths Molly had ordered; gorgeous unlit candle and flower arrangements spilled from the centers. The chairs—adorned in lush fabric and pink tulle with a sparkly jewel gathering them in the back—sat waiting for guests.

But the poster-like, colorful photos of all the stages of redoing the place Molly had taken adorned the sturdy rebuilt walls. And he'd added a massive stone fireplace—smooth with rocks from in and around the area he'd accepted from several local masons in hopes of curtailing another complete and utter disaster to that side of the building in the event of another powerful storm rolling through.

At the last minute, he'd added the images of him and Molly in the boat to be enlarged with the others—the incredible, all-telling, loving photos of them in and around the property that day where highlighted in the glossy brochures fanned out on a welcome table for the industry guests.

However, right there, in all glorious colors, their images stood on the gleaming wood mantel, proclaiming the love they shared. He couldn't stop staring at her—red hair spread out, her to-die-for blue eyes sparkling, and the achingly sweet smile on her perfect lips. He'd been lucky enough to be the guy beside her.

And he'd blown his chance again. If only he could go back…

Mrs. McCleary thrust the tux at him. "It's time."

"For what?" But he grabbed it, coming out of his stupor. "I'm sure I won't get points taken away from the visiting wedding planners, coordinators, and the local tourist industry bigwigs checking the place out if I don't dress up."

"Sean helped with the measurements. Hopefully, his memory from your football playing days and sizes line up."

Adam shook his head. "Am I supposed to have a clue here?"

"You're as stubborn as my daughter is now." She let out a loud sigh. "Do you need me to spell it out?"

"Apparently so." He looked around for help. However, Mrs. V. flittered from one table to the next, arranging place cards and adding her homemade, trademark heart-shaped cookies at each seating.

He couldn't get her attention or Mr. V.'s, who now ran a hand over the sleek bar area Adam's father was now waxing as he rubbed it down with a special cloth. And his mom and Mrs. Sanderson were going over some numbers at a tucked away table. Adam had picked up his folks at the airport earlier this morning and they were enjoying catching up with locals and receipts, it seemed.

At the mention of Molly, his heart squeezed in his chest. It had been over two long weeks without seeing her. The various people coming and going kept him updated on her whereabouts in town, appointments, photo shoots, and such. Yeah, like he needed to be reminded what he'd lost. Again.

Work and his online class finals kept his mind focused. His heart was another story altogether, though.

"Do I have to get my husband over here to have him explain this?"

"Bringing out the big guns now, Mrs. McCleary?" He'd

gone from being shunned by her, to her being an overzealous helper since the fire, and now scolding him for not wearing a tux. How had he gotten into this mess?

"It's time you married Molly!"

Adam stopped breathing as he stared at her fierce, adamant stance. The word *bulldog* came to mind. Silence blared all around him and in his ears. He hadn't been the only one shocked by her announcement.

Molly. Sweet, beautiful, funny Molly. He'd tried not to say her name, even to himself, because it hurt so much.

Every decision he'd made these last weeks were based on her suggestions, her sage advice, her stashed away files on her computer he'd found when he was at her studio weeks ago, and her wants and needs. Only she didn't know it. She'd stayed away. And he ached as he planted her lilacs and fulfilled her dreams.

Now, his blood roared back in his ears and his chest pounded, coming to life again. No, she wouldn't want this, not after how much pain he caused her.

Adam held his breath. "Tell me, Mrs. M., does your daughter know this?"

Chapter Twenty-Three

"HEY, GUYS." MOLLY waved a limp hand to her brother and Gemma as they crested the hill. They didn't answer, but she heard their footsteps coming her way.

Looking off, she tried not to see the refurbished barn from this side of the pond. With the trees cut back, straggly long limbs gone, and the heavy brush tossed, Molly stared in wonder at the sight.

On this side of the barn, Adam had painted a big red heart around the second-floor barn door. Molly clamped down on the sweet ache rushing through her.

The old rooster weathervane—tarnished in the fire—was now replaced by the gleaming metal sculpture of a cupid with a bow and arrow.

Adam's little nod to Cupid's Corner.

Molly adored it.

That was why she couldn't tear herself away from the images. Yet.

The steps halted. "Gemma to the right. Sean to the left." Molly gazed up. "Something I should know?"

Two pairs of hands reached down and grabbed her arms,

lifting her.

"Yep." Gemma turned her to face her with a stern look. "You, my friend, are coming with us. No excuses. No complaints. No hiding. Got it?"

"I was just sitting here minding my own beeswax."

"Tell us another one, Moll." Sean put his hands on her shoulders from behind.

"Wow, what's got into you two?" She gulped. "What happened to the kid gloves?"

"They're off. That's what you wanted, isn't it?" Gemma smirked. "Okay, give it to me straight, bestie. Do you still love him?"

"Adam?"

"Who else is there?" Sean and Gemma asked in unison.

"Oh, yeah. There's never been anyone other than him." Heat climbed up her neck and into her cheeks.

"That's a yes then?" Gemma refused to look away.

Searching deep inside, Molly realized she'd finally forgiven him—for the past and the present. She sucked in a shaky breath. "Still. Always. Forever."

"YOU KIDNAPPED ME to go to a non-wedding?" Molly gulped hard, finding herself facing the large, open barn door.

Her heart had expanded when they drove in and she'd spotted the final venue name Adam had selected. The new white sign with red lettering, *Cupid's Corner, Love Lives Here*, brought stunned wonder and hope to Molly.

She glanced down at her grass-stained jeans, clunky work boots, and oversized, stretched-out sweater. Brushing back her tangled hair, it didn't help one bit.

A Between Two Slices van was parked nearby. No, it couldn't be the deep fried fluffernutters the wait staff carried in those metal containers, could it? Or the chocolate ones? And the Sugar Shack van, with its back doors popped open, revealed the carefully packed tall glass jars filled with candy. The red licorice twists? Lemon drops? Wait, were those orange slices?

The local florist, Mrs. Nelson, from Petals and Blooms—yeah, the shop beside Molly's studio in town—darted in with an overflowing vase in delicate pinks and lavenders.

Could that be Martinelli's Italian restaurant delivering, too?

A wedding cake on the side of a passing white van powered out of the drive now. Even one of those five-tiered, buttercream icing ones she'd drooled over a few weeks ago?

Every piece moved with precision and purpose. Except Molly. She stood with her back plastered against the warm grill of Sean's SUV.

Gemma drew close, wrapping her arm around Molly and leaning her head on her friend's shoulder. "You know, if you didn't say you loved him we wouldn't be here."

"He had to order the little cinnamon hearts you like, Gem, right? I'm going in. Feel free to follow at any time." Sean smiled as he strolled on by, looping a garment bag over his shoulder.

"How do you put up with him?" Molly's question held a

smile.

"Him? How about the entire McCleary family? Geez. Your mom is like a bulldozer since she's been back—more so than before she left on her sabbatical. Your dad, now, he's itching to get back to work."

"Me?"

"Yeah, you know I have this amazing best friend who has no idea how strong and powerful she's always been."

"I'm just finding that out." It had taken her ages to understand her flaws and weaknesses and talents for everything they stood for and accept them. Asking for help wasn't a bad thing. Requiring someone else to do the hard stuff was. She knew the difference now.

"Good." Gemma lifted her head and gently nudged Molly. "Go forth and you shall find, or whatever that is."

"He's in there, isn't he?" The drive was clear of all personal vehicles, so nothing gave it away. She just sensed it. "I can do this, right?"

"Maybe. But you'll never find out just standing here."

"What if he, uh, dumps me again? You know, for the second time?" She gulped. The niggling fear rose up in her now.

"You could always do that to him." Gemma shoved away and tossed a knowing look over her shoulder. "Even the score? But is that who you really want to be, Moll?" She slowed down right before she entered the building.

Something curled around Molly's center and tightened. She couldn't do that to him, even pretend. He deserved better from her—then and now, with telling him how she felt.

If only she'd been brave enough to ask him to wait for her to grow up, for her to find her strength, and for both of them to tell the truth to each other.

Molly put one foot in front of the other, drawn to the need to find Adam. If nothing else, she had to tell him she forgave him. Let them both be free of those burdens once and for all.

The sun warmed her chilled body. At the threshold, she hesitated at the end of the light.

Sheer will pushed her onward into the muted sounds and unknown as she consciously crossed that barrier into the world Adam and she had created.

She blinked at the change all around her—the light bouncing off the crystals and sparkling, the honey-blond wood plank flooring, the dozens of stunningly decorated tables and chairs, the fragrant flowers tickling her senses, the delicious food, too, and the suddenly silent family and friends watching her.

Adam emerged from the back, dressed in a black tux. He came down the wide center aisle toward her, his polished dress shoes slowly and surely thudding along the boards with each step closer. "Molly…" He halted, hands curling into fists at his side.

Her heart ached for him. On shaky legs, she went to Adam, warmth flooding her body. She stopped two feet from him. "You're breathtaking."

"I thought that was the… Oh, of all things, I forgot the blender." His lips twitched upward at the corners. But it didn't shift the bruised look in his eyes.

"You make it sound like cutting up spaghetti is a crime or something." She teased him back, the band around her ribs finally easing.

"Don't tell anyone, especially the Martinellis, but I think it is."

"So, is this our seven-course meal, Adam?" Molly longed to reach out and brush back his hair, touch his face, and feel his lips again.

"Well, it couldn't get any better than deep-fried chocolate fluffernutters to start it all off, now can it?"

"Be still my hopeless romantic heart." She drew in a shaky breath like she'd gone underwater and couldn't quite gather enough air in her lungs. *I just think I flunked recovery 101.*

Adam's gaze captured hers as a smile played around his mouth. "I've missed you so much. Six years of missing you and what we had. What we could have been."

Reaching out, she touched his wrist, lifting it gently. His skin felt so warm and so good. With her left hand, she slowly unfurled his fingers, one by one. She traced a heart on his palm, like she used to in high school.

"I had to forgive me first for letting myself down when I didn't even know I had, Adam. I blamed others when I stayed hidden and didn't speak up. I can't, no, I *won't* do that anymore."

"Good. You deserve the very best. Always."

She blinked back tears and took another shuddering breath. "If we could have drowned out all those harsh thoughts about ourselves, and if we believed…just trusted in *us*, you and I would have ended up together. What I'm trying to say, Adam, is I'm so very sorry and I forgive you for hurting me."

"Why?" He took her hand and pressed it to his chest.

His heartbeat thundered under her palm. Taken aback by his fierce reaction and the heat enveloping her hand, Molly missed something. "I don't understand."

"About ending up together. Why can't we now?"

Molly shook her head, unsure, yet hopeful of what she read in his eyes now. "A second chance?" She never thought, dared hoped, for one with him…

He brushed her hair away, skimming the backs of his knuckles along her cheek, and then trailing his fingertips along her jaw. "This was all for you. My way to say sorry and giving you what I couldn't then. My way of proving I could provide for you. Proving I was good enough."

"But you were. It wasn't about *what* you could give me. It was always about *who* you were, Adam. Still are. What a good man you are to everyone"—she waved a hand to their family, friends, and neighbors who were silently rooting for them at this moment—"and how you make me feel. Beautiful and special."

"Funny, you make me feel that way, too." His lips tugged up at the corners again. "I couldn't see what you saw in me. I always belonged here. I just didn't know it. But, most importantly, I belonged to you."

Inside, Molly couldn't stop the flutters spreading through her. "Still do. I hope."

Adam sucked in a shaky breath. "Can we? Have this place and Cupid's Corner to call our home? I want to live this dream with you, Molly. I love you. I always have. Always will. Please, marry me. Here. Now."

"MOM, REALLY?" MOLLY stood before the long mirror in the bridal she-shed and held the precious wedding gown to her—not the one she'd stored away and out of sight for the last six years. That wasn't her any longer.

Somehow, Adam had discovered an image of this one she'd added to a wish list that a blushing bride would want—along with many of the touches and details he'd included in the wedding venue.

The wide band of silk coming around the front of the bodice and to the low back appeared like a thick ribbon, gathering at the base of her spine and outlining gorgeous folds of fabric and lace where they met and softly draped to the floor.

"Come on. Hurry up. Your groom is waiting."

"Thank you for realizing what's important to me, especially Adam." Molly hugged her mother. She sighed when her mom embraced her back without any coaxing. "You're getting better at these."

"Yes, well, if I have to." But she tightened her arms for another moment. "You'll have to teach me. The important things, honey."

Molly pulled away first. Freshly bathed and with her hair

in a divine updo, short nails painted a sparkly blush, and makeup done by both Grams and Gemma—because she couldn't stop her hands from shaking—Molly turned back to the dress, running a hand over the silky white fabric.

It might have taken ages to get to this point, but Adam and she would finally make their dreams come true today.

Love means I get my heart back—only wiser and stronger and filled to overflowing with more love than ever before.

Less than a half hour later, Molly strolled down the fragrant lilac pathway with her arm through her dad's while she held a beautiful, mostly white with some pale pink roses bouquet Mrs. Nelson thrust at her in the other hand.

Everyone showed their love for Adam and her with their wonderful, touching gestures and contributions to this special second chance day.

"Thanks, Daddy. For holding me up."

"Anytime, sweetheart." He dabbed his eyes with a hankie.

Gemma, in her last-minute, blush-pink maid of honor gown, took her rightful place near the makeshift altar of an arch of brilliant, colorful flowers. Adam chose Sean to be his best man—relying on their friendship from the past and their brother-in-law relationship to come.

Up ahead, the Henderson triplets—adorable in their matching dresses of white tops, red skirts with pink hearts on it and the matching capped sleeves—giggled as they flung a multitude of colorful rose petals on the ground along the way. Their dark ringlets bounced as they skipped along.

Family, friends, and hundreds of townspeople, including

Kyra and Kyle and many of Molly's engaged clients and soon-to-be wed ones in the coming weeks, stood surrounding the stone path near the heart-shaped clearing Adam had created. Bernard's flash went off too many times to count. And Mr. Pickens wore a black suit jacket and tie over his denim overalls as he stood up as the justice of the peace, having taken an online course to become one.

Molly spotted Adam as his own mom and dad— beaming with pride—fussed over his bow tie and smoothed down his lapels.

Her dad kissed her cheek goodbye and then, standing aside, guided her toward her groom.

"Hey there, handsome." Molly did a double take at what was sticking out of top front pocket on Adam's tux. "Red licorice?"

He patted it. "Just in case I lost the ring. I could always make one."

She giggled. "So creative. Who knew?"

"Gorgeous, angel." His gaze took her in and his voice cracked. "It's the tie." He smiled, his green eyes were lit from within.

Molly drew in a shivery breath as he reached down and lifted her hand. He drew a heart there.

"It feels like I've waited forever for this day."

"You, too?" She grinned through tears, her chin wobbling. "Oh, yeah, I get a little emotional at times."

With the pad of his thumb, he brushed the moisture from the corner of her lashes. "Us. Perfectly imperfect. Just the way you are is just the way I want you to be." His words resonated with conviction and a deep well of love.

"Yeah, that." Molly leaned forward and brushed her lips against his warm, sweet, firm ones. Dozens of flashes went off. Or was that fireworks in her head? Either one, it felt the same—dizzying and dreamy and tugging on her heart. Oh, that was definitely all Adam and what he did to her. *Here's to the end of recovery and onto the wonderful new beginning for the hopeless romantic in me.* "I love you, Adam Larson, yesterday, today, and forever."

"And I have always loved you, my picture-perfect bride."

The End

If you enjoyed this book, please leave a review at your favorite online retailer! Even if it's just a sentence or two it makes all the difference.

Thanks for reading *Picture Perfect Bride* by Laurie LeClair!

Discover your next romance at TulePublishing.com.

TULE
PUBLISHING

If you enjoyed *Picture Perfect Bride*,
you'll love the next book in....

The Cupid's Corner series

Book 1: *Dear Cupid*

Book 2: *Picture Perfect Bride*

Book 3: *Falling for Her*

Available now at your favorite online retailer!

More books by Laurie LeClair

The McCall Brothers Series

Book 1: *The Cowboy's Rebellious Bride*

Book 2: *The Cowboy's Renegade Bride*

Book 3: *The Cowboy's Runaway Bride*

Book 4: *The Cowboy's Christmas Bride*

Available now at your favorite online retailer!

About the Author

Bestselling author Laurie LeClair writes romantic comedy, contemporary romance, and contemporary women's fiction. Laurie's habit of daydreaming has gotten her into a few scrapes and launched her to take up her dream of writing. Finally, she can put all those stories in her head to rest as she brings them to life on the page.

Laurie considers herself a New Texan (New England born and raised and now living in Texas). She lives in Central Texas with her husband, Jim, who thankfully indulges her love of chocolate and storytelling.

Thank you for reading

Picture Perfect Bride

If you enjoyed this book, you can find more from all our great authors at TulePublishing.com, or from your favorite online retailer.

TULE
PUBLISHING

Printed in Great Britain
by Amazon